Thunder Road
And Other Stories

by
Wayne Kyle Spitzer

Contents

THUNDER ROAD

1
Spears Out

My dad used to say, "It's amazing what you can see from the back of a pickup, if you're in the right place at the right time."

For him, it was watching ash from Mt. Saint Helens darken the sky from the bed of his own father's truck in 1980—when he was just 13 years old. For me, it was watching Mt. Hood smolder and spume at precisely the same age; sitting not with my back against a rusted cab, as he had done (I knew because he had told the story a thousand times), but on the hump of a brand-new Chevrolet's wheel well—so I could keep an eye on the driver.

"I told you this was a bad idea," said Jesse, watching the man carefully, suspiciously. He held his stocking cap down so it wouldn't blow from his head. "And why the hell does he keep staring at us—me in particular?"

I watched as the old man (he had to have been at least 40) glanced at us through the rearview mirror—again. "Dunno; we're probably the first people he's seen—look around." We glanced at the spare, hardscrabble pines and the blurred, yellowed sage; the great, brown piles of basalt which littered the plain like porous turds. "Probably hasn't seen anyone alive since the Flashback."

Quint harrumphed. "No way. He would have said something." He stared through the rear window at the driver. "Probably cooks kids and feeds 'em to the dinosaurs. Or he's a pedo. I don't trust him. Not around Jess." He looked at Jesse as though the boy were fragile and needed special care. "Pretty, *pretty—*"

"Say it again," said Jesse, menacingly.

Quint hesitated. "Say what?"

"What you just said. Say it again."

Quint guffawed. "How can I say it again when I don't know what I said in the first place?" He looked at me as though he were completely nonplussed—all Quint Fucking Holloway: Innocent Man. "I don't get it. Seriously, though. What'd I say?"

"Ignore him, Miles," said Jesse. "He just wants to drag you into it."

Quint touched his fingers to his chest.

"Yeah, *you,*" said Jesse. "Peckerwood. Tornado bait. Son of a crawdaddy."

"Yo, lay off that."

"What's the matter? Your trailer wheels showing? Wood booger. Swamp Yankee. Inbredneck ..."

"Okay; it's not cute anymore," Quint growled. "Keep it up. And I swear I'll jam that stick right up your—"

"All right, knock it off, both of you. (I'd heard that in a movie once and had always wanted to say it in real life.) There's a sign coming up—what's it say? Is it Goldendale?"

The sign answered my question:

WEST 142

Goldendale

Klickitat

RIGHT ½ MILE

"Okay," I said. "This is our stop; he said he was continuing on 142." I reached for the thick, sharpened stick at my back. "Bikes ready and spears out—just in case."

We unslung our spears and stood our bikes upright. "I'll go first and you can hand the bikes down to me."

"And if he tries something?" Jesse looked at his weapon; at the clean, whittled point, which had been untested by anything—the fresh, white wood. "I mean, are we talking fight or flight? Because I'm not sure if I'm ready—"

"Flight," I said—without hesitation. I adjusted the strap of the Thermos (because that's what the lead tube looked like), feeling the sheer weight of it, the awesome responsibility. "Because—what's Hal say about unsecured places?"

"Commotions attract predators," said Jesse.

"That's right," I said.

"Unless he has a firearm," said Quint. He waved at the cab, where we saw the driver craning his neck and smiling at us—folksily, fatherly. "In which case, we *kill the son of a bitch.*"

2
Until We Meet Again

It would be incorrect to say that, without human intelligence, Goldendale simply 'lay' beneath the sun—stale, abandoned, lifeless; it didn't. To say that would be to deny what life remained: the foot-long Triassic dragonflies, for example, blue-green and iridescent, like 7-Up bottles, which erupted from the weeds as we pulled up to the market and scattered, like seeds, on the wind; or the slim, tan, almost stick-like Compies—hopping and foraging amongst street trash when we arrived—which did the same. Rather, it was that without human agency the town lived and breathed but simply *no longer knew it,* and so, far from being inert, it merely slumbered—silently, dreamlessly.

"Welcome to Goldendale," shouted the driver from his window, jocularly. "The time is half-past 65 million years B.C. and the temperature is hotter than a stolen tamale. I'd like to thank you personally for flying Hodge Worthington International and remember: the next time you fly, fly the International."

I lept out even before we'd come to a complete stop—holding my arms up to receive the bikes, snapping at Jesse and Quint to hurry.

"Whoa, whoa, *whoa,*" blurted the driver—ratcheting the brake, throwing open his door. "What's the big hurry here?"

I mounted my bike even as Jesse and Quint vaulted over the bedrail and did the same, and then we were riding away from the pickup just as fast as we could, standing on the pedals to increase our velocity, aiming for the corner of the building—the idea, I suppose, being to put its overgrown bricks between the yelling man and ourselves (in case he had a gun).

"I mean, for Pete's sake, you guys ..." He sounded wounded, exasperated. "Aren't you even going to say, *'thank you?'*"

I barked at the others to hold up and squeezed my brakes—skidding around to face him, staring at him intensely across the weed-infested, garbage-strewn lot.

"Thank you," I said. "Truly. You saved us—what?" I craned to look at Jesse, our map keeper. "About 40 miles?"

"More like 50," said Jesse. He adjusted the strap of his pack, which, like my own, had no doubt gotten heavier. "From Toppenish, and the start of 97, all the way to here. So, yeah. Thank you."

"Yeah, man. Thanks," said Quint. "Seriously."

The man moved to speak but hesitated. "Look. My name's Hodge—and I'm not a threat, all right? I promise you. I—I don't even own a weapon." He held up his arms as though to illustrate the point. "It's just that, well, I haven't seen anybody else out here. Not since Kennewick, at least, where I ... where I saw things. Terrible things. Enough to know that—whatever it is you're doing, *wherever* it is you're going ... it's a bad idea."

The wind blew, hot and cloying, and the trash skittered. Nobody said anything.

"Now you said when I picked you up that you're from a settlement; a place—a place northeast of here, up in Granger. A good place. Safe. Well, I need to tell you: there ain't no such thing as that in the cities—or out on the road—or anywhere. All right? It's just hungry lizards and hungry people, and I'd be hard-pressed to tell you which is worse. And I really think you should consider just climbing back into the bed of this truck and letting me take you home to where you came from—after I complete my business in Trout Lake, that is." He looked at us plainly, compassionately. "I'm an adult, see, a father. And that means I've got to try. Gotta try to do right by you. So what do you say?"

I looked at Jesse as the wind ruffled his collar and then to Quint, whose shoulder-length hair danced, but neither showed any emotion—nor any indication at all that their minds had been changed. I shook my head.

"There's your answer, Mr. Worthington. I'm sorry. For us, it's the Garden of Oz—or bust."

He seemed to search his memory. "The Garden of Oz ... Seems—seems I saw something about that once ... on TV, I mean. A long time ago. By—by the Hollywood sign? In Los Angeles?"

I nodded, gravely.

"What's there?"

"Our business," I said. "Just like yours—in Trout Lake."

At last he exhaled and slapped his arms against his sides, appearing to give up. "That's a thousand miles, you know; I guess you understand that. And those motocross bicycles will never make it—you understand that too?"

"We've got innertubes," I said. "And we can pick up other bikes along the way."

"Yeah, well." He scratched at his high forehead and thinning hair. "I guess you've thought of everything. Except that you're sitting ducks on those things: for highwaymen, for one—those are a thing again, you know—for raptors, for pterodactyls. But I don't suppose you're worried about any of that—being young and invulnerable, after all."

Again, nobody said anything.

The man—Hodge—looked at Jesse, appearing almost to well up. "There's a reason I kept staring at you, you know. Because you look like someone; my first son, gone long before the Flashback." He paused, seeming to choke on his words. "Like his mother, too."

I looked at Quint, who looked at Jesse—who frowned.

"All right," said Hodge. "Well. Until me meet again."

And then he climbed back into his truck and put it into gear and was gone, rumbling toward 142 which he would take west toward Trout Lake, leaving a cloud of dust. After which we thought about what he'd said—for it was obvious Jesse and Quint were doing the same—and I took out the Thermos, which we just stared at for the longest time before Quint handed me the key and I inserted it into the lid and began to turn.

* * *

3
Talon

We'd found the thing shortly after Jesse arrived at the camp (the one in Granger, a town full of dinosaur sculptures, go figure), back when we were still getting to know each other, still feeling each other out. Quint and I had already met and mostly hit it off—I'm still not sure why, he was from nearby Wapato (population 4,997) and I was from Los Angeles (I'd taken a Greyhound to spend the summer with my uncle, who had since vanished in the Flashback). We just had, same as we had with Jesse, who had arrived a short time after without so much as a knapsack—no family, no friends, nothing— and to whom we were introducing our favorite fishing spot (perfect and secluded and shady beneath the State Route 223 bridge, on the Yakima River) when the body washed up.

"Miles, what the hell is that? I mean, is that what I think it is?"

Quint sounded flabbergasted, incredulous. None of us had ever seen a dead body (aside from the disappearances, Granger had largely been spared). "Holy shit, man."

"Yeah—Jesus," said Jesse.

We laid our poles on the rocks and shuffled closer—to where it was caught up in a reed-filled shallow.

"Where's the top half of his head?"

I looked at the gaping, blue-gray mouth and plump, swollen tongue—like uncooked pork sausage—and the horseshoe mustache; above which, above a serrated edge caked in dried blood, everything was gone. "I don't know," I said. "But he died screaming."

Quint was the first to point it out: "What's *that?*"

He indicated a dull gray canister which was slung from around the thing's neck (it didn't seem proper to call it a 'man' anymore). "Look. It says something."

I inched closer, stepping into the water up to my ankles. "'Radiation Products Technology,'" I read. "It—it's like a brand-name, or something."

"Get it," said Quint.

"I'm not *touching* that thing!"

"Get it—you're right there. Don't you think Hal's going to want to look at it?" He was referring, of course, to Hal Keller, the brains behind Camp Courage's makeshift electrical system—among other things.

"Well, then Hal can come and get it," I said—and didn't budge. "What part of 'radiation' don't you understand?" I looked at the body: at the swollen tongue and horseshoe mustache—jet-black on blue— and the thing's one visible hand, which was contorted in a crook.

"I'll get it, you candy-ass," cursed Quint, and stepped into the water.

Jesse, meanwhile, had begun to stir. "Ah, guys ..."

"'Candy-ass?' What are you, my grandpa?"

Quint reached for the canister. "Hey, if the shoe fits ..."

"Ah, guys. You need to like—not move. Okay? Like, *at all."*

"Here," said Quint. "At least keep him from floating away while I—"

"If you don't shut up and hold still," growled Jesse, "we are all *going to die.* All right? Just, look south, okay? *Slowly."*

And we looked south: toward the bend in the dark, lazy river and the gray, rocky sandbars further down—and froze.

"Oh, shit," rasped Quint. "Just holy fucking shit. Is that—is that a ...?"

I waved him to silence as I studied the thing's physical makeup: the brown body and distended belly, held horizontally over the ground, like a side of beef on a spit, and the balanced tail; the wrinkled, S-curved neck; the long snout and brow horns.

"It's not good, whatever it is," I whispered. "Everyone get in the water—it hasn't seen us. *Quietly.*"

Quint demurred. "But what if—"

"Just do it. It'll help mask our smell."

And we did it, wading into the cold, (seemingly) slow-moving water, moving out deeper and deeper, something my mother had warned me against—because of the undercurrents—time and time again.

"What's the hell's it doing, anyway?" asked Jesse at last, shivering. "There's no big game around here."

I watched the therapod as it stared into the water. "It's fishing, just like we were. Probably got one in its sights. Look, see how—"

And it raised its head ... then swung it around to face us.

"Oh, shit," whined Quint. *"Oh shit-oh shit-oh shit ..."*

Nobody moved.

That's when I heard it: a kind of whisper—a *suggestion*—not vocalized *but in my mind;* as though I were thinking it to myself, as though I were imagining it.

Release us, it seemed to say. *Release us and we will protect you.*

I looked around: first at Quint and then at Jesse, both of whom seem bewildered—until my eyes settled on the corpse and its awful, gaping mouth, its frozen scream—like something from *The Thing*—and finally on to the canister, which floated and bobbed, like a buoy.

Do it, Miles.

And then it was coming—the therapod, the allosaur, *whatever*—slowly but surely; padding toward us along the bank with its eyes focused on us like laser beams, like heat-seeking missiles. Like a great cat stalking its prey.

"What are you doing?" It was Jesse—sounding alarmed. "Quint—what is he doing?"

I reached the body and gripped the canister, worked its strap up and over the corpse's partially-eaten half-head.

"Miles? What are you doing, man?" Quint, I think. "Because it's a bad idea—whatever it is. Come on. Give it to me."

"It'll protect us," I said—dreamily, dazedly. "It'll make it so that it thinks we're one of its own." It had a pin in it with a ring attached, like a hand grenade— which I pulled; but with no luck. "More, it'll let us know when there are others—other predators. We just have to release them ..."

"Jesus, stop him!"

But it was too late; I'd already twisted the ring and pulled the pin, which had opened the tube; opened it so that a weird, emerald light spilled forth even as I reached in with my fingers and felt an object—something smooth, cold, metallic, like a necklace—which I snatched up by its chain and quickly held aloft.

Something which burned like green fire as the predator entered the water but paused, snarling. Which reflected from its eyes like an emerald sun as it sniffed at the air and seemed to change its mind; as it cocked its great head—which was the size of a jet ski—in curiosity, before swinging it away like a wrecking ball and bounding from the river, back into the woods.

Something whose glow quickly faded as the threat diminished and became lifeless and inert in my hand; just a small chain with a medallion attached—which was black as coal; just a curved piece of an unknown metal (or glass) which was cold to the touch and looked like a velociraptor's scythe-like, retractable toe-claw.

Or a talon.

All of which brings us back to the present, and the fact that as Hodge drove away and I opened the Thermos a green light spilled out which painted our shirts; a light which told us—in no uncertain terms— that there was a predator (or predators) nearby. A predator—or predators—who might even then be preparing to rush us: from behind the overgrown ruins of the store, perhaps, or the Mesozoic rock formation in the street.

Or just from out of nowhere, I thought—as Hodge's truck disappeared finally down the road—*in a place that was in the middle of nowhere.*

* * *

4
Wolves of the Jurassic

I looked around: at the Les Schwab Tire Center and its sun-bleached ads (FREE BEEF WITH ANY TIRE PURCHASE!), and its block walls covered with vines; at a crusty, two-tone mobile home (beige and peapod-green) and a ruined café; a partially-collapsed house. It wasn't just that we felt like we were being watched; it was that we felt like we were being watched from every direction.

"I got a bad feeling," said Jesse—as the Talon continued to glow, to tremble. "We should—we should take cover."

"Yeah," I mumbled, warily. I resealed the Thermos and swung it around to my back. "I think you're ri—"

"That Les Schwab," said Quint. "How about that?"

I looked at its bay doors—one of which was open. "And become the free beef? Dude ... it's wide open. The market's right—"

Something rustled and we jumped—but it was just a tumbleweed, skittering across the road.

"Better think again," said Quint. "Look. Its roof is collapsed."

I looked. "It'd keep the raptors out, though. Don't you think? Maybe."

"Maybe. But it might not be raptors. It might be one of those things from Granger. Or a *whole pack.*"

"The café," said Jesse, suddenly. He indicated the overgrown—but intact—building: *The Alienated Heifer,* whatever that meant. "It'll have food—canned stuff, bottled water—if we have to hole up. Plus they'll be a walk-in—one of those big industrial freezers—in case anything gets in. Like a panic room."

We both just looked at him. The dude definitely had a knack.

"Okay," I said. "We're splitting for the diner. We are not gonna pass GO; we're not collecting 200 dollars. We're just gonna—"

"Oh, fuck," said Quint, stiffening like a board.

And we followed his gaze.

It's never easy; coming face to face with a predatory dinosaur—even one as far away as this one—especially when it just stands there like a psycho killer with its dark tail swishing slowly and its white face cocked; coldly, dispassionately—like Michael fucking Meyers. Hal says it's because they release a pheromone that causes panic and disorientation in their prey, but I think it's the eyes—which gleam like the Flashback itself (or at least the weird borealis the Flashback left behind) and can give you the heebie-jeebies. Regardless, I knew once we'd seen the Nano-A (or *Nanoallosaurus,* for I remembered its wide skull and narrow snout from Mr. Jones' science class) that we were in serious trouble; for it was, or had been, or was again, amongst the deadliest of predators: a smart, lithe species Jones had referred to as—because of its sophisticated pack behavior—"the Wolves of the Jurassic."

"Nobody move," I said. "Just—don't even breathe." I reached for the Thermos and brought it around. "There's something about this. Something—"

"Forget it," said Quint. He indicated the Nano-A. "I don't want to get close to that thing. Besides, we don't even know if it'll work—the Talon, I mean. It could have been a fluke. No way, man. We need to run, *now.*"

I opened the canister and took out the Talon, which glowed, fiercely.

"He's right," said Jesse. "You're putting too much faith in that." He shielded his eyes and looked at the diner. "We can make it but only if we get a head start. And that means getting a move on it; like, right—"

He jumped as something cried out—we all did—like a fisher cat at night; or a drunken woman shouting unintelligibly.

"Jesus," said Quint. "What the hell was *that?*"

"It came from the other side of the market," said Jesse. "Whatever it was."

I put the Talon around my neck. "It's what I'm trying to tell you, there isn't just ..." I trailed off, suddenly, looking for the Nano-A. "Where'd it go?"

We all just looked at the spot.

"Okay, fuck this," said Quint—and dumped his bike.

"Yeah," said Jesse—doing the same. "For once we agree."

"But don't you see, running might be just exactly—"

And then Jesse was grabbing my arm and I was dumping my bike (as well as the thermos) and we were all of us breaking into a sprint—just bolting toward the diner like lunatics, like frightened children, which I guess we were, leaping across the pavement in bounds—even as I glanced at a nearby fence and saw the tumbleweed from earlier pushed right up against it—rocking and vibrating and shaking, as though it were alive—deposited there by the wind; trapped.

* * *

5
Wane

They say your entire life flashes before your eyes right before you die, but that's not what happened—not to me, anyway. Instead, I found myself thinking about all the people closest to me that weren't actually there (not including my parents, oddly enough): people like Hal Keller, who would have been sitting down to a cold lunch of hot mustard sardines and boiled water—if he bothered to eat at all—at Camp Courage about then; or Macey McNeil—who was probably so worried about us she *couldn't* eat, much less teach, or Colby Higgins, listening to the Stones' "Hang Fire" on his shitty cassette deck (for the millionth time) while sipping that godawful herbal tea of his and tending his marijuana plants. And it seemed to me these images all had one thing in common—which was that they all showed just how wonderful otherwise mundane post-apocalyptic life could actually be; how smooth it could run if one just had the good sense to accept things and to appreciate them and to let the dead or disappeared or just plain missing lie; to not tempt fortune on some foolish, ill-conceived, even suicidal, errand; *to stay put.*

To live to see one's 14th birthday—which seemed unlikely now that the animals had begun appearing from everywhere: from corners and recesses and stands of dry, prickly hawthorns; from the dark between buildings and the cover of stalled, faded vehicles. From everywhere and nowhere at once: triangulating us, boxing us in, choking off our every escape—until one of them tripped over a toppled motorcycle and, falling on its saurian ass, provided us the opening we needed.

And then we were through; we'd threaded the noose and piled through the café's front door, closing it behind us, and the dark-blue predators with their ghostly white faces could only howl and gnash their teeth as we braced it with red vinyl booth benches and finally a cigarette machine—which, to our surprise, held the thing firm; even after they'd started butting it with their heads (at least, I assume that's what they were doing).

"See? *See?*" Quint sounded manic, unhinged; hysterical. "If we'd relied on the Talon we'd be *dead* right now ..."

I looked down and closed my hand about it, wondering why it felt different (at least from before), why it shone dimmer. Why it died completely even as I touched it.

"All right, never mind, spears out," said Quint—as if from a million miles away.

Maybe they weren't close enough, I thought. Sure; the thing at the river had practically been on top of us. Or maybe—maybe it *attracted* them first; that is, before finally repelling them. But that wouldn't explain the loss of—

"Come on, come on!"

I looked at the shaking door and the red, vinyl booth seats; the rattling, old-fashioned cigarette machine with its clear glass pull-knobs and LUCKY STRIKES masthead—like something from the '50s. Or maybe its energy had simply had a lifespan—like everything and everyone else—and was just gone now; extinguished; like my parents, most likely, like the world.

"Goddammit, Miles!"

And then I was awake; I was back in the moment—holding my spear, standing with my friends. Then I was ready to die fighting as the glass of the door shattered and a swinging head wormed in and its jaws snapped open and closed and its teeth gnashed; as Quint drove his spear through its maw and out the back of its skull—where it ran with blood and brains—and another took its place; and hand-like talons, white as the things' faces, began to reach and grope and feel about—like the arms of cats, I

supposed, so eerily articulate and human—like
shambling fucking zombies.

* * *

6
Interlude

I don't how long it took to finally ward them off: maybe 50 seconds, maybe 5 minutes—all I know is that by the time they retreated to their partially-collapsed buildings and stands of hoary hawthorns we were utterly and thoroughly wasted; I mean trashed, and just collapsed in heaps right there on the floor—on the black and white checkered tile of *The Alienated Heifer.*

"Jesus," gasped Quint. "Just ... I thought we were goners. Like, serious goners." He rolled over onto his back and exhaled, explosively. "I gotta hand it to you; you guys rallied like sons of bitches." He laughed suddenly, boisterously, which became a coughing jag. "Wouldn't believe it if I hadn't seen it myself."

I looked at Jesse—who was on his hands and knees next to me—in time to see his reaction, which wasn't pleased.

"Yeah? Well, sub-divide me and Kentucky-fry me, is that a backhanded compliment—from *you, Quint?"*

"Yo, *eat shit, man ..."*

"Yo, how 'bout we skip the catfight?" I rubbed the bridge of my nose and looked at them. "Until we know what's going on. Yeah?"

I dragged myself to the nearest window and pulled myself up, then peeked between the blinds.

"Well?" said Jesse.

I scanned the lot; from the hawthorn trees approximately west of us to the beige and pea-green shit-fest (the two-tone manufactured home) northeast.

"Nothing," I said. "Or at least, nothing obvious." I let out a sigh. "I think they might actually—wait; wait a minute." I studied the lattice fencing around what passed for a deck. "Right there. There's one behind that fencing ... real low ... sly." Jesse sidled up next to me as I reexamined the lot and the fresh market across the street. "And right there—behind that truck. See it?"

"I see it," he said. "Also there—behind the garden soil."

We turned and pressed our backs against the wall.

"We're not going anywhere," I said—even as my eyes came to rest on Quint. "Not for a good while."

"Yeah, well." He stretched and stared at the ceiling, as though he were thinking about something else. "We needed a break, anyway." He let out a sigh.

Nobody said anything.

"Jesse," he said, all mock earnest-like. "Tell me a story."

I glanced at Jesse—expecting fireworks—but he only shook his head: Forget it. And then we just stared ahead: close enough to kiss but saying nothing, as though we were straddling urinals.

At last, he said, "Do you suppose I really look like that guy's son—Hodge, I mean?"

I gazed at a framed print on the wall: a surprised-looking cow standing aloof from the herd—caught in a U.F.O's tractor beam. "I don't—I don't see why not. He seemed earnest enough. I mean, what do you think?"

"I don't know ..." He exhaled slowly, deliberately. "I didn't see any resemblance between him and me. I know that much." He leaned forward with his elbows on his knees. "It's funny; he could have been my own father ... and I'd have never known it." He laughed a little. "But then Hodge seemed to actually care."

I looked at him but didn't say anything.

At last, I said, "Must be tough, not having known your parents. But, you know, probably not a day goes by—that they don't think about you. You know?" I shifted and leaned forward—so I could see his face. "You ever think about that?"

He just shook his head. "Would that be before or after they dropped me off at the social services office?"

I locked his brown eyes up in my own. "Before *and* after. And every day after that ... for the rest of their lives."

He looked at me doubtfully and I raised an eyebrow. "Wanna bet?"

And then he smiled—even shoved me in the shoulder. "Yeah; how about a hundred now-worthless dollars?"

"Two-hundred," I said, and kept eye contact. "*Sand* dollars. When we get to the ocean."

I watched as his smile began to fade and he leaned back against the wall.

"Do you really think we'll make it—all the way to L.A.?"

I just stared at him and took a deep breath, then let it out.

"I do," I said. "I have faith ... in that much, at least."

"And your parents?"

But I just shook my head. "I don't know."

And then we let it go, as we had let go of so many other things, as Hal and Macey and Colby (and yes, even Quint) had let go; as had the billions who'd vanished, who'd died—as had everything; even Time itself.

7

Dumb like a Fox

"What about you? Why'd you come?"

I looked from Jesse, who'd asked the question, to Quint, who'd sat up on an elbow to watch us.

"What?"

"What about you? I mean, we know why Miles is here; he wants to know what happened to his parents. And we know why *I'm* here—I don't have anything else to lose. But why are you? I mean, you lost your parents, right? So are we here for the same reason; that we don't have anything else to lose? Or is it something else?" He added quickly: "I'm bonding with you, Quint. Help us read the entrails."

To my surprise, Quint actually seemed to think about it.

"I'm here to lend muscle," he said—determinedly, and sat up in a huff. "I mean, let's face it, you two—" He left off abruptly, as though reconsidering his words. "What I mean is ... we were just brought up differently, that's all."

"Oh? How's that?" But I knew what he meant: He meant he hadn't grown up with a silver spoon in his mouth, like me, or coddled by the state, like Jesse.

"Yeah," said Jesse. "Explain it."

"Look, I'd rather not, okay?" He shoved off the floor and began pacing—slowly, deliberately, like a tiger in a cage. "I mean, I didn't grow up in some blue heaven yupscale People's Republic of—*wherever,* if that's what you mean." He stopped and leaned against the lunch counter, facing away from us—toward the kitchen. "I grew up in Wapato; where the only education you get is the free trade and vocational school of high-toned son of a bitch old men, like my dad." He paused as though humbled, even ashamed. "You know ... the one where they teach you how to fly a flag and shoot at beer cans; or win an all-American fight, or tailgate old ladies while laying on the horn."

He stood straight suddenly and squared his shoulders. "I guess what I'm saying is, that I have some attributes. Ones that might just help us to stay alive—even if they're not always pretty. Miles—Miles seemed like he needed that. When he mentioned the trip, I mean."

Again, there was silence.

"How do you do that?"

He turned and just looked at me. "What?"

"How do you win an all-American fight?" I must have glanced at my shoes because I remember noticing how scuffed and threadbare they were, how worn out.

"You sucker punch him—and then you *just keep punching him;* just batter him like a hockey player, until he's good and down."

I looked at Jesse and he looked back. "And then—what? Do you help him up?"

"You start kicking. You just kick the living shit out of him. In the face, in the teeth—until someone tells you to stop."

"Oh. And … and if he sucker punches you first?"

"He won't. Because he won't know he's in a fight." He hitched up his Rustler jeans and knelt beside the barricade—like a coach, I thought, or a drill sergeant, then tapped his right temple. "Because, *attributes.*"

"Yeah, well," said Jesse. "Thank you. But those attributes suck. And they're dumb."

But he just smiled at us rakishly, almost dashingly, and at Jesse in particular. "Yeah? Okay. So I'm dumb—just a dumb kid, really. Like all of us. But then, unlike you," He winked at him with a piercing blue eye—which struck me as unusual. "I'm dumb like a fox."

And the two just stared at each other—which, I have to say, was weird as shit. But, well, there it is. I reckoned that for Jesse and Quint, mere friendship just wasn't ever going to be in the cards (or the entrails).

And boy, was I right.

* * *

8
Demon and Machine

"Dude, Miles. Come on, man, wake up."

I stirred where I'd fallen asleep beneath the window (for I was still engaged with my mother, who had come to me in a dream), wondering why it was so bright out (it had been late afternoon when I'd started to nod), why Jesse was shaking me. "Don't. Just ... *Would you leave me alone?*"

I sat up with a start—having just realized where the light was coming from—and covered the Talon with my hand. "Holy shit. I mean, just, *holy shit. Dude. It's back.*"

I looked at Quint, who had fallen asleep beneath the lunch counter, and then at Jesse, who was beside himself with terror. "What—what is it? What's going on?"

He placed a hand on my shoulder and peeked between the blinds, which rattled softly. "I mean—you tell me."

I shifted around and joined him, still waking up, then peered through the gap. "I don't see anything. Just the tire shop and the fresh mar—wait. Something just moved. See that? Right there—behind that Subaru."

"That's Machine," said Jesse. "He's the Alpha. Mean bastard, by the looks of him, and a lot bigger than the rest. He's the one to watch—the 25th grizzly, as they say."

I must have looked confused.

"'The kind of bear that tolerates no man or bear; one that will maul without bias.'" He shrugged as though it wasn't important, just something he'd said. "I saw it on the Discovery Channel. And over there," He slid his finger along the dusty blind, toward a truck. "That's Demon. Because of her brow horns."

He shook the hair from his eyes and glanced at me. "I've been watching and naming them—while you guys slept. Most of them have been hanging back; Machine seems to want it that way, based on his vocalizations. But he and Demon, they just keep coming—ever since the Talon woke up. Like it's a dino magnet or something. Like they're attracted to it."

"They are," I said—not knowing how I knew it, only that I did. And then I reached for the Thermos—only to recall, quite suddenly, that I'd dropped it. That I'd dumped it in my panic just like my bike, and that there was no way to shield the

Talon's power now. That—now that it was back on—there was no way to turn it off.

I looked at the door and the stacked red benches, and the cigarette machine, which had been pushed back by the animals (about six inches, but still). "Bigger, you say. Like, how much bigger?"

"A lot," said Jesse. "Like, 50 percent, at least. Like it's not even the same species."

I stood and began backing away. "We've got to find the walk-in, something with good, thick walls—or a basement." I kicked Quint in the feet—hard. "Get up."

"There is one—a basement, I mean," said Jesse. "Found it while you guys were sleeping. I—*oh, fuck.*"

"What? What is it?"

"It's Machine—he's on the move." He released the blinds and looked at me. "On the move and heading this way. Fast."

"Fuck ..."

"Follow me," said Jesse. "Hurry."

And we did, hurry, that is, dragging Quint who was barely awake and snatching up our spears; shoving through the swinging doors into the filthy, cobwebbed kitchen, piling downstairs into the musty darkness even as Machine collided with the front door and wood splintered and broke and there was a tremendous smashing noise which could only have been the cigarette machine falling over and its glass breaking.

Which could only have been the diner being breached as the sun continued to sink and twilight fell; as our hearts pounded in our chests like pistons, like drums, and I ran back up the steps to close the door.

* * *

9
Basic White Teenage Boy

I took the Talon from around my neck and dropped it in the dust. "Hurry up," I said. "Cover it with something, anything. Those bags of flour."

I started dragging the sacks from the shelves and letting them fall to the floor—as Jesse and Quint lifted the 50-pound bags together and threw them over the Talon, which cut off our light.

"Whatever happened to just letting it repel the bastards?" asked Quint, and grunted. "I mean, at this point, it's pretty much just a liability, don't you think?"

"Yeah, sure." I took off my pack and started digging for my lighter. "You gonna be the one to wear it? It's like you said: I don't even want to be close to those things."

"We should ditch it, then," said Quint. "That is, if we ever get out of this mess."

"No," I snapped, remembering the voice, and the way it had repelled the dinosaur on the Yakima River. "It—it's still our best bet if we get caught in the open. And it—it means something. I tell you. It's important."

"Yeah," said Quint. "Important at getting us killed."

I flicked on my lighter, having found it amongst the tools in the small pouch of my pack, even as pots and pans reigned down—clattering and clanging—somewhere above.

"It's in the kitchen," said Jesse. "Machine, I mean. And Demon too, I bet. Oh, shit—Miles. What are we going to do?"

I looked around the basement: at the industrial-sized cans of tomato sauce and 5-gallon buckets of dish soap; at the 50-pound bags of corn starch, the cans and cans of coffee beans. "Who am I to know," I said—and extinguished the lighter. It was getting hot. "I'm just your basic white teenage boy." I looked at Quint; or at least where I thought he was. "Why don't you ask 'Dumb like a Fox?'"

Jesse didn't miss a beat. "Hey, Dumb like a Fox, what do ya got?"

But Quint didn't say anything—only remained silent as the animal or animals above brushed against the basement door, snorting and sniffing and snarling.

"Quint?"

Which is when we heard it: a drizzling and a spattering, like a thin stream of water. A dribbling and a dripping—percolating in the dust. "I'm pissing, if you don't mind," he said at last—and added: "Back here, in a sort of cubby."

"Well, hurry up," I snapped. "We've got to figure a way out of this cluster—"

"Yo, Miles," he said. "Bring your lighter over here." I heard a rustling and a swishing, like small boxes being moved around. "Just—just follow my voice."

I gripped the lighter and followed his voice ... to where he was standing in the dark before a high set of shelves; shelves packed with a hundred different types of boxes and tubes—all of them colorful, all of them garish.

To be honest, it took me a minute to realize what I was looking at. "I don't ... I mean ... Are those—?"

He grabbed a clear package of what appeared almost to be shotgun shells and held them out between us. "And no; *you ain't imagining things.*" He gave the package a little heft. "How many sticks of dynamite in this?"

"None," I said, as Jesse joined us, and moved the lighter farther away. "That's—that's an urban legend. Those are just flash powder; black powder. They're not quarter sticks of dynamite."

Quint studied the cherry bombs, the M-80s. "Yeah, but—whatever. They'll make a big boom, won't they?"

I looked at all the boxes and tubes and other packages: shelf after shelf after shelf of them, like our own private fireworks stand. Our own little—or not so little—artillery depot.

"Oh, yeah," I said—and held out my free hand, palm up.

At which they slapped it; first Quint—way too hard, I might add—and then Jesse.

And we went to work.

* * *

10
Fuse

"All right, you dogs, *roll call,*" shouted Quint—gruffly, briskly, like a true leatherneck. "Alpha Battalion is 'go' for launch—and I mean *hot to trot.* I repeat: I am 'go' for launch. Bravo Company—sound off like you got a pair."

Quint and I waited: Nothing. Not so much as a peep.

At last, Jesse said, in a voice deeper than usual: "Yes—*yes, sir!*" He laughed. "Bravo Company standing by! And hot to trot, *sir!*"

"Better late than never," said Quint—like a disappointed drill instructor—before adding, "Okay, faster now, more intense: Forward-Battalion Charlie—*let's hear it.*"

"Sir, yes, sir!"

I took up my position at the base of the stairs—having just come down from loosening the doorknob—watching the entrance to the basement like a hawk; crouching over my rockets and missiles like a villain, like Wile E. Coyote. "Charlie Company—I mean Battalion, is ready to rock and roll, *sir!*" I bumped the flashlight and had to reposition it—so it again illuminated the fireworks. "And will fire on your command—sir!"

I braced myself as the creature—"Machine"—snorted and nudged open the door, which creaked and moaned. "And that should probably come sooner rather than later—if you know what I mean; and I think you do. And enough of this 'sir' shit ..."

And then we all just looked at each other: Jesse and Quint from their places at the window wells (they'd climbed atop 5-gallon buckets to reach them), each with their own rockets, and me by the stairs—by the Talon, which was now covered with only a single bag of flour, for easy retrieval.

"Be sure to light *everything;* like, every fuse in your arsenal," I reminded them. "Just—go all in. Then it's straight for the bikes ... all right? Everyone got that?"

Jesse just nodded, somberly. "And then what, do you think?"

"We put the Talon back in the Thermos and we *ride,* all the way to the Columbia River and beyond—to the Dalles, at least. And we don't stop until we're safe; like, in a hotel or something. On the very top floor."

Quint seemed to think about it. "Yeah, but—we stop at the river ... just for a while. You know—to hang out."

"To *hang out?*" I could see Jesse's exasperation from across the room—even in the dark, or the semi-dark. "And do *what,* exactly? In case you were wondering, there are, like, *dinosaurs* out there. Or haven't you noticed?"

"I don't know—maybe ... maybe swim, or something. I just—look, I've never seen a river. All right?"

The admission knocked me back—even though there were predators at our very door. And I remember thinking, *Jesus, I know there are people who have never seen the ocean—but a river?* It was slightly funny and somehow heartbreaking all at the same time. I mean, Christ; what kind of people had his parents been?

"Okay, we're stopping at the river," I said. "Biggs Junction, I think it was called, across the U.S. 97 bridge. We'll—we'll celebrate. Break out some cans of tuna, or something. For Quint's first river—and it's a doozy."

"What are we waiting for, then," said Quint. "Let's do it."

"Okay," I said. "On the count of three. You ready? One ... two ..."

There was a snarling sound and I looked at the door: saw Demon and Machine jerking and thrashing against each other violently (they'd poked their heads through at the same time and managed to get stuck; like Archie and Meathead). And now they were blocking the door completely—blocking our way out.

"Wait a minute," I shouted. "Wait a minute ...!"

Whereupon, to my complete and utter surprise, they pulled free of the frame, and—in a riot of busting glass and clanging kitchenware—began to fight; to just tear each other apart, right there in the kitchen—at which our pathway opened again like the gates of Heaven and I barked, vociferously: "Okay, do it; *do it, do it, do it!*"

And we began to flick our lighters—desperately. Frenziedly.

* * *

11
Finale

I'd be hard-pressed to describe the bedlam that followed—and rapidly doubled, tripled, quadrupled—other than to say that what started humbly, subtly, innocuously, with a chorus of staggered hisses and frizzles, quickly became a cannonade; a fusillade, a barrage of such sound and fury and color that, had I not been so focused on lighting fuses, would surely have blinded me, at least temporarily. As it was, I was able to launch virtually everything before ricocheting rockets forced me to shelter in place (which is to say, with one skinny arm thrown over my exposed head and shoulders); after which, cowering, I could only cough and hack in the stifling smoke—all while praying nothing detonated too close. Which, as it turned out, nothing did. And, also, that the warring dinosaurs had fled. Which—as it turned out—they had.

"Jesse! Quint! Long-fuses!" I rolled the 50-pound bag off the Talon. "And remember: Straight for the bikes!" (I was referring, of course, to the special fuses we'd made; which—it was hoped—would provide cover after we left.)

"That's a negative, hombre," shouted Quint. "I'm fresh out of lighter fluid over here." He quickly added: "Jesse! Get over here!"

"No!" I barked. "Belay that order! Keep up your barrage ..."

And I was on my way, bounding for Quint and holding up my lighter, shaking it, impatiently, as he turned and just stared at it—disoriented, shell-shocked. (Some of my rockets had—after ricocheting about wildly—blown up right next to him.)

"Take it!" I snapped—even as a ghost-white snout lunged at him through the window, lunged at him and crashed to a halt—snarling, gnashing its teeth; at which Quint spun upon it and clocked it in the nose, *hard,* and just kept clocking—until it yelped and beat a retreat.

"Okay," I said, "go, go, go!" And he took the lighter.

And then I could only return to the Talon and snatch it up off the floor, noting its fading color, its waning strength, before swinging it around my head and barking, "There's never going to be a better time. How much more?"

"Just about," said Jesse, and continued: "Just—okay! Okay, I'm clear!"

I looked at Quint, who was still lighting. "All right, forget it, let 'em go ..."

He moved the lighter from one fuse to the next. "Hold on," he said, "just hold on ..."

At which we could only watch, rocking on our feet, hopping up and down, until he lit the last fuse and jumped down from the bucket.

And then we were hustling—double-timing it, as they say—up the stairs and out of the diner, where not a single predator could be seen. Then we were scrambling for our bikes; our pinto horses of plastic and steel; which gleamed like salvation even as the long-fused rockets began to explode and the Nano-As, active but in hiding, began to whimper and howl.

That's when I knew it; when I could feel it in my bones: That we'd passed our first test; survived our baptism by fire. That's when I knew that our journey would be complete—as we sat on our bikes with our spears canted at our backs (like the bows of Indian braves, I fancied) and, having returned the Talon to its canister, watched the last of the fireworks as they burst and boomed above. Watched, brooding, as they turned the sky first white then green then blue, and finally, a deep, lingering red, after which, taking a cue from our fellow animals, we began to howl ourselves.

* * *

12
The Mighty Columbo

I think it's safe to say we all know the scene: it's the one in *Jurassic Park* where Dr. Alan Grant—having just been informed that billionaire John Hammond has successfully recreated a T. rex—begins teetering about like a drunkard before eventually collapsing in the grass and looking on, dramatically—at the towering brachiosaurs as they wade across a small, glittering lake; at a herd of parasaurolophuses drinking in the shimmering, south American heat; at the birds fluttering about the sauropods' great bodies. Well, that's a little what it was like as we gazed out at the Columbia River from the Sam Hill Memorial Bridge: like something from the movies, from *Jurassic Park,* complete with long-necked sauropods (I think these were diplodocuses) drinking along the dry, rocky banks, and pterodactyls gathered on their broad, silver backs. Even the air was shimmering; I suppose because, although the sun showed only 10:00, it was already getting hot.

"So this is the—the Columbo River?" Quint tried not to sound too impressed. "But it's just a lake, like on *Fishin' with the Good Ol' Boys.* It doesn't even move." He added: "Fuck it—all the better to swim in, right?"

"It moves, you just can't see it," I said. "There are currents—trust me. Same as with any river." I looked at the brachiosaurs and then down into the silvery depths. "Besides, dude, seriously. Who knows what's down there."

"I'm not afraid of any currents," said Quint. "Or prehistoric fish." He stood and straddled his bike. "I'll jump in right here. We all should."

"Yeah?" said Jesse. "In what? Our birthday suits?"

Quint just looked at him. "Why not? What—you afraid somebody will see your weenie? Dude. Nobody cares. *Come on.*"

"I'm not getting in that water."

"But it's the great and storied Columbo Lake!" He glanced at me as if to gauge my reaction (I'd been talking the thing up for the last 13 miles). "I mean river."

I guess my smile must have faded (I had been studying him keenly in the hope he might experience some sort of epiphany: about crossing thresholds, maybe, like Joseph Campbell talked about, or just appreciating the beauty and splendor of the natural world—or unnatural, as the case may be—and our diminutive place in it). *"That's*

Columbia," I said. "It's called the Columbia." I peered down the length of the bridge to the rust-brown truss and beyond—all the way to Biggs Junction, which was just a smear of buildings. "And across the river is Oregon; the, ah, Beaver State. Which we should be getting to."

"The Beaver State?" Quint reoriented himself to face south. "Well—hell, why didn't you say so. I'm there, dude." He splayed his arms above his head as though worshiping a deity. "I have found my homeland!"

"That's not what he meant," said Jesse. "Besides, you won't—you wouldn't have liked it. At all. Neither you nor your old man. Before the Flashback, I mean."

"Yeah? Why not?"

"Big lib state," he said—and began peddling away.

He called back: "You couldn't even pump your own gas!"

And we just watched him—ride off, that is—not straight as an arrow, not aggressively, like Quint or I, but weaving, meandering.

"Is that true?" asked Quint, turning to look at me. "That you couldn't pump your own gas? Why?"

I shrugged, continuing to watch Jesse. "Beats me. Could have been a holdover—something from the '50s. How am I to know? Probably wasn't as safe back then—pumping gas, I mean."

"*Mm,*" said Quint, and laughed. "He's right, though. The old man would have had a heart attack; being told he couldn't pump his own gas." He added out of nowhere: "But he's wrong to just lump us together. Me and my old man, I mean. We—we weren't the same. Not really. He's wrong about that."

I turned to look at him, struck by his sudden candor—saw the same look in his eye I'd noticed at the diner, the same self-awareness. "Yeah, well," I said. "It takes two to tangle. Maybe you should—"

"So are you," he added—shutting me down. And then he kicked off for the truss, for the State of Oregon; for Jesse, at which I could only gaze at the river and wonder—again—at that weird moment between them (the one in the diner); that moment when they'd just stared at each other like they might kill each other on the spot. When reality itself had seemed to stretch—to warp—to shift its very meaning; and I'd felt as though I were seeing something which, like the change in my voice or the rapid growth in my legs, had only now been born—only now come into existence. A moment of rapid and unexpected change.

I looked at the weird borealis the Flashback had left behind—it was purple and blood-red today—and the strange lights that flickered deep within its depths.

Just a moment. Like a hologram, I thought, which changed depending on which angle you viewed it from. Or Schrodinger's Cat. Or the Flashback itself: indecipherable, unfathomable, non-sensical. Absurd.

And then I put my bike in gear and followed them—my traveling companions. My bickering quest-mates who would never change; whom I didn't want to change.

My only friends in the world.

* * *

13
Benson Bridge

I don't know why we stared at that dead pterodactyl chick so long—there wasn't anything particularly striking or even gross about it; there were no flies, for example, no maggots—just a couple of butterflies, one white and the other burnt orange, which matched the fading sunlight.

Maybe it was our nonstop ride all the way from Biggs Junction near the Washington border to Multnomah Falls, which was closer to Portland (I mean, it's a lot of work, peddling a BMX bicycle some 70-plus miles, even across level terrain). Or maybe it was how paper-thin the creature's exsanguinous, oyster-white skin was, how almost translucent, or the way its little talons weren't really talons at all but little hands, like a baby's hands. All I remember for certain is how contemplative everyone seemed to get while looking down at it—how funereal; even elegiac—like we were saying goodbye to one of our own. All I remember for certain is something akin to holding vigil for a fellow traveler; which, in a very real sense, we were.

"For him, the war is over," I whispered—although I doubt anyone heard me over the crash and roar of the falls. "I wonder where Mom is ..."

"Not here, that's for sure," said Quint. "There are no nests."

I followed his gaze into the treetops and beyond, to the waterfall itself, which dashed and cascaded down the cliffs. "Weird. I mean—where the hell could it have come from?"

"Maybe it came from up there," said Jesse. "From the very top. There's—there's a platform up there, a wooden observation deck. We came here on a field trip once and hiked up to it. Be a good place to build a nest—real stable. And defensible."

I looked from one end of the concrete bridge—"Benson Bridge," the sign had called it—which was closed off with cyclone fencing, to the other. "Speaking of which, this bridge looks pretty defensible—don't you think?" I peered off the way we had come. "Only one side to protect; we can take turns standing watch ... I mean, it may not be the Ritz but—what do you say?"

We looked around and then at each other.

"Hell, I'm in," said Quint. "We can even build a fire and maybe eat something—something hot, I mean. It'll be just like—it'll be just like Camp Courage!"

I couldn't help but to notice he'd stopped short of saying "home," and a quick glance at Jesse confirmed he'd noticed it too; although whether he'd done so because his own home life had sucked or because he'd understood—in that moment—that, because of the Flashback, we'd never see home again, I don't know.

"Sure, why not," said Jesse. "We can heat up that beef stew, the one we were saving for Portland. We're close enough." He shrugged off his pack and spear and laid down his bike. "And besides, it'll lighten my load."

He dug out the can of Dinty Moore stew and paused, looking at it. "Seems ... almost wasteful, though ... doesn't it? I mean ... you'd like to think, you'd like to think nothing was born ... just to lay there and rot, you know?"

We all turned to look at the bird.

"Yeah," said Quint. "I mean, it's like God laid it out there just for us, and here we are wanting to eat something from a can."

I got off my bike and reached for my pocketknife—touched its smooth, imitation-wood handle. "We're going to have to learn how to hunt eventually, I suppose. I mean—"

"I already know how to hunt," said Quint.

"And to clean and dress a—"

"I know how to do that, too." He held out his hand for my knife—which I gave over to him: slowly, reluctantly. "And since both you pussies missed man-school; I guess I'll be the one to have to show you."

Jesse looked at me and then back to Quint. "Let me guess. Because—attributes."

"Because—attributes," said Quint, and got off his bike.

* * *

14
Roast Pterodactyl

As it turned out—it was actually pretty good: closer to duck, I think, than anything else; more red meat than white, coppery and gamey, with a generous layer of fat. As for how it paired with warm Mountain Dew—well, you might be surprised; but then anything can be good with the right company and the right circumstances, which, as I took stock of the crackling fire and unfurled sleeping bags, the defensive wire comprised of cyclone fencing and canted spears, the raging waterfall, the serene moon—I knew these to be. You just had to be in a certain frame of mind; a certain mood; or to have survived something most people your age hadn't.

"And now," said Quint, letting out a belch, "a moment of reflection." He dug through his bag and pulled something out; something long and narrowish and wrapped in cellophane. "Brough to you by— Swisher Sweets!"

I looked at Jesse and he looked back—then back again to the package of cigars. I didn't know where he'd gotten them, probably from the bureau in Colby Higgins' pimped out, tie-dyed cabin tent; all I knew for certain was that a cigar sounded positively titillating at that moment—that slice of time not even the Flashback could touch—even though I'd never had one and had no idea how to smoke it; nor even what to expect.

"Hit me," I said, even as Quint mockingly cocked a fist, then held out my hand as he quickly tore open the package.

"Yeah'um," said Jesse. "Me, too. Hit me, that is."

And he handed us each a cigar.

Now, there is little that hasn't already been said about one's first experience with smoking, especially when one has the misfortunate of accidentally inhaling, and I mean straight away. You could say that it stabs you like so many knives through the chest even as it bites deep into your lungs; that there's a sense of breathing and *not* breathing even as the smoke swirls and seems to expand; that there's a buzzing in your brain and your senses are dulled, like you've suffered a blow to the head. Most of that would be true, to a greater or lesser extent (it was certainly true for me, as I hacked and coughed and spit). And yet one of these was not true: which was that, far from being dulled, my senses had, in fact, been *heightened*. Sharpened. Indeed, after the wheezing had stopped and I'd grown accustomed to the buzz; after the stars and galaxies had snapped into focus (including the arm of the Milky Way itself) and a calm had settled over me like a down blanket in winter—and I'd learned how to puff (without inhaling) and even to make smoke rings—I dare say the experience became—*enjoyable.* Amiable.

Sublime.

"See?" said Quint. "That's what *I'm* talking about."

"Yep," said Jesse. He puffed and blew a huge cloud of smoke. "After a day spent fighting dinosaurs and riding, like, 73 miles—ain't nothin' like a good cigar."

I shifted to look at the Borealis, which was a deep, stunning cobalt tonight, a kind of alien, darkling blue, and the equally strange lights within. "They're vaguely geometrical—you ever notice that? Like triangles—sort of. Or arrowheads. I don't think they're intelligently controlled. Not by pilots, I mean."

"What's it matter?" sneered Quint. "I mean, anyone who could have figured it out is probably long gone by now; either disappeared in the Flashback or eaten by reptiles. Nah," He poked at the fire listlessly, lackadaisically. "We ain't *never* gonna know. No more than they knew how to cure cancer; or stop the aging process. Or cure a common cold. Forget about it."

"Forget about it, he says," I muttered, and reached for the Thermos, which I'd placed away from the fire. "Sure, why not." I turned the thing over in my hands, watching the firelight play across its curved, silvery surface. "But then, there's one thing I can't forget."

"Yeah?" He puffed his cheeks out and blew a series of smoke rings. "And what's that?"

I pitched the canister to him and he caught it, sort of, fumbling it in his lap.

"It's your turn to carry this."

And then I stubbed out my cigar and rolled up in my sleeping bag, not thinking about how the Talon had beckoned to me on the Yakima River or how it had referred to itself as "we" rather than an "I"—or that it had referred to itself at all—or about how it could burn so brightly one minute and lay utterly inert the next, or that I might just be fucking crazy, or about anything, really, not even my parents.

And then I just tuned out: curling up and shutting my eyes—clearing my thoughts; letting it all go.

Forgetting about it.

* * *

15
The Garden of Oz

It was funny: that I should have thought earlier on the fact that we could never go home—for when I awakened (or at least partially awakened), blinking my eyes and watching the curtains rustle, smelling the sweet lilacs in the Garden of Oz, well, I realized I had done just that.

Gone home.

"That's it, Miles," coaxed my mother, softly, encouragingly, urgently. "We need you to wake up; okay? Need you here, and present—and alert. Come on, honey."

I rolled to face her and found her sitting on the bed next to me—pensively, I thought; broodingly, her hair having fallen partly over her face. "I can smell lilacs," I said, and sniffed at the air. "But it's already late July."

She swiped the hair out of her eyes and regarded me. "And do you like it? The way their smell just sort of permeates the house and makes the sunlight itself seem lavender? Is that how you remember it?"

I lay and just stared at her. Then I nodded. "And the tourists ... laughing. Having a good time.

Some of them from as far away as China. All of them having come *here*—to a place we already live. Or live next to." I studied her face, the faint lines around her eyes. "The Garden of Oz. L.A.'s oasis of beauty and whimsey and green, as Dad would say. The best place to have grown up in the world; even if it's in what President Tucker called a liberal—can I curse, Mom?"

"I know what he said."

I shrugged the thought away. "A place where people found something they needed. That's what I remember."

"Then what does it matter?" She cupped my cheek in her slim, soft hand; which was cool to the touch. "Late July, early May. In-season, out-of-season. It's just time, Miles. It isn't, and never has been, for us to hold to the task. Now—come. I need to show you something."

And she pulled away and stood—calmly, stoically, before gliding wordlessly to the door and vanishing into the hall, at which I threw off the blankets and quickly followed.

Nor had the house changed much—if at all—it was still as regal as it was airy with its eggshell-blue walls and whiter than white wainscoting; its wide backyard in which sheets fluttered restlessly—tempestuously—from the clothesline; like flags from a gantline.

"Mom ... *hey!*"

But she didn't stop, only continued toward the hung laundry, toward the undulating sheets, her pace quickening, her long, dark hair billowing—until she'd reached them at last and, to my complete and utter astonishment, passed directly *through them.* Just vanished without a trace.

"Mom!" I cried, even as I crashed into the sheets myself and fought them off; as I emerged onto the other side but could only look on in horror.

As I noticed sudden movement and looked toward the gazebo—where a pack of velociraptors had descended on my dad even as he'd tried to mow the lawn. Where they'd split him head to crotch and unspooled his entrails—and were eating him alive—as the sheets snapped behind me and the wind blew and I awakened again to find Jesse bleeding from the throat and hanging onto the side of the bridge.

Where I saw him trying to call out but only managing a gargle as the great, dark pterodactyl—its wings beating furiously—attempted to carry him off; to steal him away, even as Quint and I rallied but were too late and the thing rose into the purple dawn like a dragon—like some great vampire bat; gripping its struggling cargo like a vise, flying up and up and up.

Taking him to its massive nest—which, as we could now clearly see (and as Jesse had predicted), lie at the very top of the falls.

* * *

16
Left Behind

John Gardner once wrote, in deference to the human condition and its limitations (as well as its delusions), "But they rush across chasms on spiderwebs, and sometimes they make it, and that, they think, settles that!"

Well, that's essentially what Quint did when he swung across that ravine—having lept for one of the gnarled vines and somehow made it (even as I skidded to a halt at the edge of the cliff and teetered). He'd dashed across the chasm on a spiderweb. He'd done precisely what Quint Holloway always did: which was to seize an opportunity before anyone even knew it by acting without a care or forethought (nor the slightest concern for his safety) and with the gravest of intent. To the point that I felt feckless and impotent as he casually dropped the vine (which had broken off as he swung) and hurried up the trail, not so much as looking back. To the point that I could only curse to myself in frustration as I stood there looking at the remaining plants (all of which were too short and/or flimsy to even attempt such a move) and found myself wishing—not for the first time, and certainly not the last—that I, too, were dumb like a fox, or had fucking "attributes."

And then I was backing away in order to get a fresh start and launching myself at the crevice like a madman—like a fool. Then I was bounding over it like some kind of superhero even as my momentum flagged and I fell distinctly short—bouncing and sliding down the rocks like a rag doll, like a sack of blood and bone; tumbling into the pit like a cadaver—where I lay broken and bleeding; and still. Where I saw Quint helping Jesse out of the nest and the two embracing like lovers, like comrades (even as Mama-bird continued the hunt elsewhere and her chicks snapped and squealed). Saw them as though I were looking through the Talon itself, which I now realized Quint had taken out and put around his neck.

Where I saw and heard things I couldn't possibly have been able to experience—at least not from so far away—before finally passing out. At which, somewhere in the depths, I heard a cool, sinewy voice say, simply: *Now you've seen as we see.*

As it turned out, I wasn't nearly so banged up as I thought; which we found out after they'd fished me out of the crack in the earth and patched me up (we had a First-Aid kit in one of the bags, just a little tin box with Band-Aids, sterile pads, gauze, and gloves). Hell, I hadn't even sprained anything, which was pretty miraculous considering the tumble I'd taken. Quint, for one, was impressed.

"I gotta hand it to you, kid. You're as tough as a box of nails." He glanced at Jesse, who'd needed sprucing up himself. "And *you.*" He swung the Thermos—in which he'd replaced the Talon—around to his back. "I thought you were a goner. Jesus. What a ride."

"I ... it ..." Jesse pointed at the gauze wrapped around his throat. "It hurts to talk. But ... Thanks. Thanks for coming after me."

Quint just shrugged. "What are friends for—if not to rescue you from a pterodactyl nest at zero-dark thirty in the morning?" And they laughed—or at least tried to—after which Quint extended his hand. "No hard feelings, okay?"

"No hard feelings," rasped Jesse.

I watched as his thin, callow hand met Quint's— which was so much blockier, stubbier—before finally looking away: to the northern horizon and its craggy, basalt cliffs; to the silvery band of river and its overgrown parking lot—where a single vehicle could be seen through the framing of the trees; a vehicle I was pretty sure hadn't been there before.

A pickup, I realized, as I squinted and studied the truck. One that was oddly familiar now that—

"Jesse: How far is Trout Lake from Multnomah Falls?"

"I don't know," said Jesse. "About, what, fifty miles? I'd have to look at the map. They're in the same vicinity, I remember that."

I peered at the truck, which shone clean and new and unblemished, as though it had just been driven from the lot.

"Well, I'll be goddamned," I said. And then I turned toward the others. "Gentlemen—what do you say we go down there and say hello to an old friend?"

* * *

17
A Bigger Gun

Had the weather not changed so much after we passed through Portland—and Jesse and I not moved into the cab of the truck (while Quint stayed outside in the bed with an umbrella, because, in his words, he was an "outdoor dog"), I doubt we would have gotten to know Hodge any better than the last time we'd bumped into him.

As it was, we did a lot more than just get to know him; we fell in love with him a little, I think—or at least came to care for him in a way only those who have experienced a great hardship (like a World War, say, or a genocide, or a Flashback) can: by which I mean quickly and without hesitation; based on a bond rather than pure circumstance. By which I mean without any pretense or conditioning whatever—because there simply wasn't room for it, wasn't the time. There never had been.

None of which changed the fact that, after nearly five hours and 300 miles, his "Hodge Worthington Airlines" shtick—which had never been funny—was starting to grate: even if he only lapsed into it on occasion; like when we merged onto US Route 101 from WV 42 and he said, "And now, if you'll kindly look to your right, you will see the magnificent *Pacific Ocean;* or at least, you *would* see it—if not for the rain and fog."

I looked out my window into the great, gray void, and shook my head. "Tough break for Quint. His first ocean—and you can't even see the bloody thing."

Jesse only poured over his maps. "He'll have lots of time; we're going to be next to it pretty much the rest of the way." He glanced over his shoulder into the payload area. "But you know Mr. Attributes. He'll probably be disappointed." He lapsed into a serviceable impression of Quint: "Where's the big waves, like on *Hawaii Five-O?* Where's all the pirate ships?"

I laughed and looked around him, at Hodge. "So you really think you're going to find anyone in Wolf Creek?"

Hodge merely shrugged, focusing on the road. "It doesn't really matter if I do or not. You know? The point is, I have to try. These people were my friends; they were an important part of my life—right up until the end, right up until the Flashback. If I don't look for them now—when they might desperately need my help—how the hell much did I care to begin with?" He glanced through the rearview mirror at Quint; who was just the top of an umbrella. "I learned a long time ago: friendship's just a word—if it's never tested. If it's never put to the fire. It'll be the same with you: with you and Jesse, and with Quint. If you don't know that yet; you will."

"Yeah, but ..." Jesse scrutinized the map he was holding. "Didn't you say you were heading east—at Ophir? A little past Port Orford?"

"That's right," said Hodge. "On Skunks Misery Road—just a little past Prehistoric Gardens." He chuckled a little at the thought of it. "Prehistoric Gardens. Ha. Think about *that* one."

"Yeah, but. There's nothing there," said Jesse. "No road at all. Just the edge of a mountain range— the Klamath Mountains."

Hodge only laughed. "Not on your map, aye?" He smiled to himself warmly. "No, I guess it wouldn't be. Speaking of which,"

He slowed down as we approached a sign: a sign bearing a brown stegosaurus which read, in large, hand-painted letters:

HERE!

PREHISTORIC GARDENS

IN *Oregon's*

RAIN FOREST

"See the gift shop? You can ride out the storm there."

He pulled up next to a goofy-looking T-rex statue and came to a stop. "Unless of course you want to forget all this nonsense and just come with me. Because this is it; this is my last stop. After this, it's northeast to Montana, where I hear there's a settlement. But I can drop you in Granger along the way."

I opened the passenger-side door but paused, looking at him around Jesse. "This friend of yours—in Wolf Creek. He might just as well be alive as dead or vanished—huh?"

Hodge didn't say anything; only rummaged around behind his seat.

"Is it nonsense to want to find out which one?"

He dug out a black, hard-plastic case and handed it to Jesse; the weight of which lowered his arms. "Look—I get it. Okay? I'm not here to judge. But I do want you to have this." He patted the case where it sat in Jesse's lap. "If what you told me about Quint is true, he'll know what to do with it. Have him show you—*both* of you. Okay?"

He stared straight ahead through the wipers and the rain. "Now get out of here; before I start carrying on about my son—and about how Jesse reminds me of him. Go on. *Git.*"

And we got, climbing out into the storm even as Quint tossed out our packs and spears and handed down our bikes; taking refuge beneath the giftshop's eve as Hodge backed up and drove away and Jesse handed Quint the case; which he opened to reveal a large, scoped handgun and various accessories—including ammunition. Which he took out and gave a heft even as Hodge's taillights disappeared and there was a deep, guttural roar, a great, rumbling bellow; which rose up from the nearby trees like thunder even as we tried the door and found it unlocked, and quickly shuffled in.

As we huddled in the cold and dark and the gargantuan sound came again—vibrating the floor, rattling the panes; and Jesse said—in the most unwelcome attempt at humor *ever:* "We're going to need a bigger gun."

* * *

18
Exit Through the Gift Shop

"Okay, this is where the fun begins, so listen up," said Quint. "The first thing you're gonna do is to open the cylinder—like this."

He slid the cylinder lock forward and pushed the spindle out, which clicked, softly. "Right? Okay?"

"Got it," I said.

"Mm," said Jesse.

Quint moved to load the gun—a stainless steel Smith and Wesson which was so new it gleamed; I mean it positively shined—but paused. "Jesse? You got it?"

Jesse shifted in the doorway of the shop—which was wide enough to hold us all. "Slide the cylinder lock forward ... then push the cylinder out. Got it," he said.

"Okay." Quint turned his palm up—which was full of copper rounds. "Now we're gonna load it. Just slide each of them into a chamber—like that—rotate the cylinder ... close it, and lock it into place." He looked from me to Jesse, earnestly, gravely. "Now which of you is going to cover me?"

I stared at the gun before looking at Jesse—who only shook his head, slowly, solemnly—and then back to Quint. "I'll do it," I said. "If you show me how—"

"Let's start with your stance," he interrupted; and pointed the pistol at the ground. "But first I want to show you how to pass this thing." I watched as he reopened the cylinder and stuck his thumb through the revolver—then slowly handed it to me. "Got that? You don't just say, 'Here—take this,' and hand it over. Always make sure the cylinder is out and you're pointed at the ground. Okay? Now close it up."

I hesitated, acclimating myself to the heft and feel of the thing; wondering if I was remotely ready; keeping it pointed at the ground—then pushed the cylinder shut and locked the spindle in place. "Okay," I said.

"Now spread your feet ... a little wider, wider than your shoulders; good. Bend your knees—no, no, just a little. Stick your butt out. Just a little. Now bend forward ..."

Jesse laughed—and I shot him a look.

"Focus ... all right. Good. Now," He pretended like he was holding the gun. "The way you fire this beast is pretty simple: your shooting hand goes around the handle like—well, like that, actually; just be sure to keep your finger out of the guard until it's

time to shoot; and your support hand goes—yep, just like that, over your fingers. And then you're going to extend your arms ... come on, bring 'em up ... and you're going to take your left thumb—no, no; *dude,* your *left* thumb—and you're going to *slowly* bring back the hammer—just nice and easy—until it locks."

There was a ratcheting sound as the cylinder rotated once and stopped. "Just like that." Then he laid a hand on my shoulder and gave it a pat. "And that—believe it or not—is all it takes. You're ready to unleash hell. Or at least to cover me while I place the Talon."

I squeezed an eye shut even as I sighted the T. rex statue; as I sighted its huge, green iris (just as Quint would try to sight whatever had made that roar later—if our plan worked, that is) and my body veritably trembled. As Quint guided my aim away gently but firmly and pointed me toward a pile of wood and debris. "No, bud. That rex is concrete; it'll ricochet. Shoot at the lumber. And remember—squeeze, don't pull. And get ready for the kickback. It's a Magnum."

But I didn't fire; choosing instead to hold the hammer with my thumb even as I squeezed the trigger and lowered the hammer slowly, carefully, so that the gun became un-cocked. After which I looked at Quint and said, "We shouldn't waste rounds. Besides, I'm good—I know what to expect. Go place the Talon. I got you covered."

And then I added (noticing the way he was looking at me, just sort of slack-jawed and flabbergasted): "Seen it on TV—about a million times—and wanted to try it myself. It—it works good."

At which Quint swung the leather strap of the Thermos over his head and moved out into the dirt parking lot—pausing once to look at me over his shoulder; speechless for the first time since I'd met him.

* * *

19
Giganotosaur

It's possible I'd heard them even before awakening—before fighting my way up from dream—the dull, cumbersome impacts; like the slack being taken up from a freight train; the *kroom, kroom, kroom,* like distant (but approaching) thunder. All I know for certain is that by the time I'd sat up they were literally vibrating the windows—rattling the glassware—enough that I found it hard to believe anyone (much less Jesse and Quint, who, like me, had learned to sleep light) could slumber through it.

Enough, I suppose, that I somehow knew what was coming even before it lumbered onto the lot and paused, sniffing. For what I saw there was nothing short of *Giganotosaurus carolinii*—which, like *Nano-allosaurus,* I remembered from Mr. Jones' science class. What I saw there was something so positively mind-bending; so very nearly Lovecraftian in its size and shape and scope, that I completely ignored the plan (which was to have Quint take the fatal shot) and reached for the pistol myself; all but ensuring that our goal of attracting the thing with the Talon (which now hung from a fencepost at the far end of the lot) before killing it straight away through its soft, supple eye—would fail. And fail it did; spectacularly. *Bloodily,* in a sense.

For that was the moment in which it approached the Talon and I scoped its eye—its keen, yellow, *lolling* eye—but then did something inexplicable, unforgivable; something Quint would never have done.

I hesitated. Worse; I *cowered*—even going so far as to lay the gun on the sill as the Talon slowly faded and the giganotosaur grew restless; sniffing the air. Even, I dare say, retreating—as the beast seemed to detect something and slowly turned to face us; then charged without warning, snarling and bellowing. As it collided with the gift shop and its walls began tumbling and Quint and Jesse were awakened—rudely; as it roared and the latter began shouting, hysterically, "It's me! It's me! Oh—*don't you see? It's after me!*" before fleeing—desperately, frenziedly, finally—into the damp, crepuscular, post-storm night.

And then we ran after him—just ran, through the moist rain forest and past the crude, gray statue of a triceratops; past an ankylosaurus and a trachodon, over a low, decorative fence into the woods. Nor was the giganotosaur far—for we could hear its breathing and the gnashing of its teeth even as it pursued us through the trees and the dripping ferns and shrubs; as we burst out onto a moonlit beach and saw Jesse entering the tide, advancing up to his waist. As the giganotosaur emerged with the sound of busting timber and roared too close behind us—too close, by far.

"Go, go, go!" I shouted, putting on a burst of speed, following Quint into the water, into the ocean, which breathed like a giant, advancing up to my neck in the freezing froth and spray. "It's all right! It's okay! I—I don't think it swims. Everybody—everybody just chill." I looked at Jesse, who locked his brown eyes up in my own. "It—it's going to be all right. *Okay?*"

And then we all looked at the giganotosaur—the tyrannosaurus rex on steroids, the beast to end all beasts, and saw that, indeed, it *had* avoided the water—and that it was avoiding it still; and more, that it was sniffing at the air randomly, almost blindly—as though it had lost our scent; as though it had lost our trail.

As though it couldn't see us—at which it swung its great head around to look behind it (as though maybe it had erred and we were somehow back there), and, after wringing its little hands in frustration (or a very close approximation) pivoted abruptly—and left.

At which, seeing that we were safe (at least for the moment), and still, remarkably, in one piece, we did what any self-respecting mammal would do: we capered and frolicked and splashed like fools—and tackled each other amidst the salt and foam. Or rather Quint and I did even as Jesse looked on: wary, silent. Demur.

* * *

<h1 style="text-align:center">20</h1>
<h1 style="text-align:center">Blood Brothers</h1>

Nor did Jesse leave the water when we did, choosing instead—inexplicably—to stay behind, submerged up to his neck, shivering.

"Dude, what?" I paused at the edge of the tide.

"Nothing," he said, and trembled. "It's just that—that thing could still be out there. Just—just waiting for us. You know?"

"Dude,"

"He's not worried about that," growled Quint, stepping up next to me.

"Oh, I'm not?" Jesse glowered at him. "Then what am I doing? Just, you know, catching hypothermia—for the hell of it? It's out there, I'm tell—"

"No," said Quint, flatly. "Because getting in the water took care of it—didn't it?"

"Jesus, Quint." I looked at him, surprised. "Cut the guy some—"

"He knows what I'm talking about," said Quint—and unzipped his jacket. "Don't you, Jesse? Or is that even your real name? Same as he knows that he can't leave the water because his clothes are wet. And we'll see his ... Look—forget it. Here, take this,"

He walked back into the tide, extending his coat.

Because getting in the water took care of it—didn't it?

Same as he knows that he can't leave the water because his clothes are wet. And we'll see his ...

And that's when it hit me. That's when the full extent of my stupidity and cluelessness came rushing in—came swinging like a sledgehammer (because, apparently, that's what it took to get my attention). That's when the *obviousness* of it struck me like a bludgeon—a proverbial club upside the head—a fucking hammer.

Blood.

Menstrual blood.

Hadn't people believed once that it could attract predators, namely sharks and bears? And even if that had been disproven—and I was pretty sure it had—wasn't it at least possible that predatory dinosaurs might be the exception; especially since some species (like T. rex) were believed to have had exceptional olfactory capabilities? And if *that* were the case, how far-fetched was it, really, that giganotosaurus—and possibly others—might have been attracted to ...

"Oh, Jesus."

I looked at Jesse.

"I mean, just ..." And then I retched—harshly, repeatedly, as though I'd just gotten off the VelociCoaster at Universal (as in fact I had, retched, that is, when I'd gotten off the coaster—on that last trip to Florida, the one right before the Flashback).

Then I threw up—as though I'd been taken for one helluva ride.

"What?" Jesse spat. "Sorry I'm not one of the boys? Is that it?"

I shook my head. "No ... I ... it's just that ..."

"Blame it on my mom; it was her idea," said Jesse—even as her teeth clattered and Quint approached with the coat. As the ocean roared and the moon shone, coolly, dispassionately. "Before she got divested of her intestines—by a pack of velociraptors. She, she didn't think a woman could be safe—after the Flashback, I mean. And she was right ... from what I witnessed on my way to Granger. Before I got to Camp Courage." She looked through her wet hair at us. "Before Hal and Macey—and Colby. And you. Both of you."

I watched, disoriented, as Quint draped the jacket over her shoulders—then helped her toward shore. "But ... I mean," I stammered. *"Quint.* How did ... How long—"

"How long have I known?" He stooped to pick up Jesse's hat. "I didn't. Not until a few minutes ago." He wrung the hat out and handed it to her. "But I've suspected from the beginning—if you want to know the truth." He paused, staring at her hand, the palm of which was bloodied. "What happened?"

"Nothing," she said. "I—I fell in the woods. That's all."

"But it is something," I said, not really knowing what I meant, trying to figure it out. "Because you got that while trying to help us—while trying to lure the thing away; whether you were conscious of it or not. And the reason you did that was simple—you did it because we're brothers." I looked from her to Quint and then back again. "And when one of us bleeds, we all do."

And then I took out my knife and extended its blade—examining its edge, examining my friends. Then I drew it across my palm so that the blood welled up instantly and, staring into Jesse's eyes, held my hand out to her.

The tide rolled in and back out again.

"We all do," she agreed—and clasped it firmly, un-waveringly. "Together we stand. No matter what."

"No matter what," said Quint—having cut his own palm—then gripped hands with each of us in turn. "Together we stand—and may nothing tear us apart. That's our vow."

"Our vow," repeated Jesse, staring up at him.

And then it was done and we were heading back: back toward the gift shop—or what was left of it—and our packs which contained dry clothes; back to our bikes and spears and the Talon—as well as our quest to learn what happened to my parents—along the beckoning, barren Thunder Road.

URBAN DECAY

Each of us, I think, had to understand it on our own terms, the totality of the desolation, the speed at which the old world had fallen away. Each of us, I think, had something of an epiphany looking down at it.

For me, it was seeing the helicopter's shadow slink wraith-like over the hulk-jammed freeways and overgrown downtown intersections, realizing that shadow was the only thing—the only *human* thing—moving in any direction. For Sam it may have been the aircraft carrier—the *USS Nimitz*, Roman had said—run aground between Pike Street Market and the big Ferris wheel (and presumably straight into the State Route 99 tunnel). Leastwise that's what she was looking at as she gasped audibly and the helicopter swung north by north-east, over what would have been Belltown, toward the Space Needle.

"You gotta see this," said Roman, his voice sounding generic, condensed, tinny over the headsets. "Anyone here ever seen an eagle's nest? In the wild, I mean?"

Lazaro hmphed. "I've scaled a 200-foot Douglas fir and touched one. Does that count?"

Nigel sneered—you could actually *hear* it, even from the front. "Ya, mon. But only in your dreams."

Roman nodded at Lazaro. "Yeah? Was it big?" He sounded jocular, condescending. "How big was it, you think?"

"I don't know. About four feet," said Lazaro. He seemed annoyed—even hurt. "What's it matter?"

"I was just wondering how it compared to, say, that, at five o'clock."

We all saw it at once as the helicopter leaned and I was pressed against Sam: a nest the size of one of those above-ground pools—the kind someone like Lazaro might have had before the Flashback—built up around the Needle's radio tower and comprised of what appeared to be mud and fallen timber.

"Jesus, it's everywhere," whispered Sam, her face and chesnut-brown hair—which smelled of honeysuckle and gunpowder—reflected in the glass. "They—they're blue, *teal.* Like robins' eggs." She shook her head pensively, meditatively. "I wouldn't have thought that."

"Where's momma bird?" said Lazaro.

"That's a good question," muttered Roman. He made a complete circuit of the Needle before leaving its orbit completely and heading back in the direction we'd come. "Nor are we sticking around to find out." He voice became suddenly focused. "Okay. I'm going to fly low between the buildings—because you can bet we're being watched. So, don't freak out. The idea is to shield our location from prying eyes for as long as possible—or at least until the chopper's up and everyone is clear. Got it?"

Check. Downtown Seattle was not a safe place, especially in the business district, and not just because there were pterodactyls roosting in the skyscrapers. For one, it bordered on territory controlled by the Skidders, a ruthless gang which operated out of Doc Maynard's Public House and Underground Tour in Pioneer Square. It also shared a border with New Beijing and a group called the Gang of Four. Neither, Roman had assured us, were to be trifled with, and both were known to make frequent excursions into the no-man's land of the business district. Throw in roving packs of velociraptors, which were also territorial, or the occasional tyrannosaurid, or even an herbivore with the Flashback in its eyes, and you had a situation which needed to be gotten into and gotten out of quickly.

And *quietly.*

"Just *stay in range,*" I said, checking the switch of my walkie-talkie, making certain it was on. "Or it'll be a shitshow all over again."

It was a cheap remark—no one had been closer to Chives than Roman—and one I regretted immediately. "No," he said, and crossed himself. "It won't. Trust me. Anything bigger than an alley cat—

you're going to know it. We'll get you inside, I promise."

"It's not getting inside I'm worried about. It's getting *out* with what we came for."

He looked at me with those damned earnest eyes—something I would have preferred he didn't do, especially while thundering between skyscrapers—and smiled. "We'll do that, too. Now lock and load, Jamie. All of you. We're almost there."

"See that courtyard just east of the library? That's our landing zone," said Roman, slowing us to a near hover, beginning to lower altitude.

I watched as the helicopter's shadow grew on the wild, waving grass.

"Again: when you hit dirt I want you to go immediately to the street—5th Avenue, right there, and follow it south-west. Stay close to the buildings, they'll give you some cover. Get ready."

"From predators?" asked Joan, our mechanic, her voice full of doubt. It was her first time out of the compound with us.

"From *people,*" said Roman. "They've been known to snipe from the towers." We touched down with a slight bounce—tall grass lashing at the windows. "Remember, right on Marion ... then all the way to 1st—to the Exchange Building. You can't miss it: there's a Starbucks across the street with a—"

Joan balked. "There must be a hundred—"

"... with a gutted triceratops in its window." He looked at her over his shoulder, then at each of us individually. "It's—it's probably been picked clean by now." He swallowed as though he'd said too much, then straightened suddenly and nodded once. "Everyone just—stay sharp, okay? Good luck."

And then we were moving, piling out of the hatch and into the prop-wash, scrambling for the street, as the Bell 206 climbed—the sound of its rotors thundering, reverberating off the buildings, the grass dancing.

"Other side of the intersection, that condo," I said, "let's go."

We double-timed across the pavement—or what was left of it—to where a concrete overhang offered some measure of cover.

"Hold up," said Nigel. He dropped to his knees and began assembling his weapon—a commercial weed trimmer outfitted with a 10" saw blade—as Lazaro hovered above him.

"Yeah, hold up. Nigel saw some grass he wants to trim," said Lazaro.

Nigel primed the trimmer but didn't start it. "I didn't hear you complain when this opened the belly of that Barney—you know the one that had you pinned? Or did you forget about that?"

"And covered me with its guts," said Lazaro. He pumped his shotgun briskly. "You were too close. Charlene would have taken you both."

"That so, mon? Like it took Chives?"

I glanced at Lazaro and saw him bunching a fist. "Stand down, Lazaro ... I said stand down! Now!" I looked at the others quickly, hoping to quell any unrest. "We all know precisely what happened to Chives ... and there ain't nothing—I mean nothing— that is going to change that. Ever." I made eye contact with Nigel as he stood. "He couldn't be left that way. Period. Now let's move—Lazaro, take point. Nigel, bring up the rear. Let's go."

And we went, hustling down 5th Avenue even as the sky grumbled and it began to spit rain—all the way to Marion Street, at which we turned right ... and were promptly greeted by a hail of gunfire.

At first it had seemed like a miracle, the fact that there was an underground garage opening right there and that we'd all managed to get into it before anybody was hit—at least until the metal gate came rattling down and we realized our attackers hadn't so much targeted us as *herded* us directly into a trap.

"Drop 'em, now!" came a voice, even as we spun in its direction and raised our weapons—and quickly realized there was nothing to shoot at. Nothing visible, at any rate. What there was, however, were tiny red dots—on our foreheads, over our hearts.

"You see them. Good," said the voice, just as cool as iced tea—the perfect accompaniment to the clatter of shifting firearms. "And now you're going to bend down ... slowly ... and lay all your weapons at your feet. All right? *Nooo* one has to get hurt. Just do as I say ... and then we can have a nice conversation. About who you are, for example. And where you're from. And what you're doing being dropped off by a helicopter in the middle of disputed territory. Our territory. Okay?"

"Okay," I said, and nodded at the others—and at Lazaro twice; we'd been in this situation before and he always wanted to play chicken.

Slowly everyone did it—the red dots never wavering, the rain starting to rattle against the gate.

"Is that a *weed* wacker?" said the voice, and was followed by laughter. "Damn."

I heard the tapping of what turned out to be an axe head against concrete before I realized he'd stepped into a shaft of gray light. "Don't let their laughter get to you—people used to laugh at us too."

We watched, paralyzed, as the bearded silhouette seemed to yawn and stretch. "What can I say? All this rain—it makes me sleepy. I'll tell you, I could really go for a Flat White about now. Two ristretto espresso shots, some whole milk steamed to perfection, a little ephemeral latte art right in the center. Sounds good, doesn't it?" He cocked his head in the near perfect silence. "No? What you want then, a bronson? At this hour? A good, earthy black IPA, perhaps? I could go for that. Something with a nice malty backbone—good for the old ticker." He laughed, seeming to think about it. "I know. Too conventional, right?" He shook his head. "Momma always said: she said, 'Atticus, all your taste is in your mouth.'"

There was a thin chuckle and a few clanks of the axe. "Kind of mean, don't you think? Anyway. That's what she said."

He began walking toward us—slowly, deliberately—dragging the handle, dragging its blade along the pavement.

"Look," I said. "We didn't come here looking for any ..."

"Any what?" He stopped about four feet in front of me, close enough at last for us to have a good look at him, and what we saw seemed utterly incongruous with what Roman had told us—except, of course, for the multitude of tattoos (mostly triangles), and even more so the washboarded scar, which ran from somewhere on his scalp and through an eye (over which one lens of his dark, plastic-framed glasses had been painted black) clear to his left shoulder. That much, at least, fit. What didn't fit was the slicked-back pompadour and long, full, meticulously-trimmed beard—Jesus, there was even product in it—nor, for that matter, the flannel lumberjack shirt and skinny jeans, not to mention the Converse sneakers. What didn't fit, as the similarly attired men holding laser-guided rifles emerged from behind overgrown automobiles and support columns, was that the feared and formidable Skidders were, when exposed to the light of day (and not to put too fine a point on it), *hipsters.*

"Well doesn't this just take the cake," said Lazaro, and spit.

"I take it we aren't what you expected," said Atticus. He leaned on the axe as though it were a cane. "I must say, neither are you." His good eye, which was a pale, piercing blue, dropped to our weapons. "You came well-armed. What are those—M4s? Not exactly an easy thing to come by—since Big Green fled the scene." He raised his chin and cocked his head, studying us. "And that helicopter. I mean, *damn.* What did you do? Raid a small airport? Got a pilot, even."

He began pacing, slowly, methodically. "That's better than a doctor. So, to summarize: You got a helicopter. You got military-issue rifles. You got, well, plumbing—I mean, you're clean, all of you. You even got ..." He stopped dead in his tracks, dead in front of Sam. "You even got—a girl!" He screwed up his face suddenly and leaned back, staring at Joan, who glowered at him. "Make that plural. Sorry. It's just that ..." He looked Sam up and down. "It isn't always this easy to tell—"

"Look, what do you want?" I snapped.

Atticus reared his head back as though he'd been wounded. "Jesus! Tone. I was just going to say how important it is for the fairer sex to be represented in any post-apocalyptic scenario. You know, women." He leaned close to me, I have no idea why. "My boys call them tassels—fuck if I know. Something out of Williamsburg, I suppose. Like putting crayons in your beard, or whatever." He stepped back to address us all. "All of which is just my way of saying—you have a home. A base. A place to hang your hat. And because of that, I've only got two questions." He hefted the axe suddenly and decisively—before switching it to his other hand and touching it to the ground. "Where? And why, since you have your own turf, would you come prancing onto ours—a crime punishable by death? I mean, just, holy bugfuck. It had to be for something good, right?"

"What's it matter if you're just going to kill us anyway?" protested Lazaro. "You said it yourself: 'a crime punishable by death.' So why should we tell you anything?"

"Because information is currency," said Atticus flatly. He added quickly: "One I might just accept in exchange for your lives. Along with your guns, of course. And maybe the girl. It really all depends on the quality of your—"

But I'd stopped listening: focusing instead on the darkness behind him, behind his men. Because something had moved there. Something amongst the cars.

Several somethings.

"The pharmacy," I interrupted quickly, almost breathlessly, "the one on Madison Street. B-Bartell Drugs. That's—that's where we were going." I looked sidelong at Sam as sweat beaded along my brow. "We were going to Bartell Drugs—for prenatal vitamins. I'm sorry, Sam."

"That's very interesting," said Atticus, matter-of-factly. "But considering we're on Marion I'd say you overshot the mark."

I stared at Sam intensely, trying to communicate in secret, trying to communicate with my eyes alone. "We—couldn't get to it from there. There were raptors between us and it; at least, that's what I think they were. They—they were in some kind of utility tunnel, which was dark. I'm the only one who saw them. The others—they, they had to take my word.

We we're looping around the building to bypass the tunnel when you opened fire." Sam faced forward again and squinted, her expression a mask, her composure unwavering. That's when *I* knew *she* knew.

"As for the guns—take them," I said, trying not to look into the dark. "Just let us get the supplements. Please."

I looked to find Atticus staring at me, his head at an angle, his mouth hanging open. Then he guffawed—once, twice—and paced away, raising the axe head as he did so, slapping the flat of its blade against his palm. *"Man.* You are one *noble* fuck. *All of you.* And here I thought you were just a bunch of hardened, cutthroat survivors—come to take a slice of our purloined pie, no doubt." He stopped suddenly and turned around. "You, with the wire-frame glasses. Raptor-spotter. What's your name, son?"

I glanced at Sam on one side and Nigel on the other.

"Jamie," I said, and looked at my shoes. "Jamie Klein."

"Jamie," he repeated, and approached to within a few feet. "Jamie Klein." He pinched the axe between his knees as he began to swing and stretch his arms. "Damn. That suits you, you know? I mean, you seem like a nice guy. A real mensch. Are you Jewish?"

I shook my head.

"No. Well, it's not important. What is important is that we establish a baseline. Something that, well, will get me the truth—when I ask a simple, goddamn question. So I'm going to ask you one more time, before I give the word. Where is your base-camp? And why—you need to think about this, you might even say your life depends on it—have you come to Pioneer Square?"

"I told you," I said. "We needed medicine and supplements for—"

"The girl," he said, and took a step back—even as two of his men (who weren't training rifles) grabbed Sam by the upper arms and forced her to the pavement.

"Sorry about this, troops—I really am. But I did say it: You needed to think about this one. Carefully." He took up the axe and tapped its head on the pavement. "I mean, you don't get to be the Big Dog without keeping your word, right?" He raised the hatchet slowly, confidently, the leather of his half gloves crinkling. "And believe me when I say: When it comes to south Seattle, we *are* the Big Dog ..."

That's when something leapt up in the darkness and my eyes darted to the blur—in time to see a blue and red velociraptor pounce the farthest Skidder back: its sickle-foot claws latching firmly into his abdomen, its fore-talons gripping his broad, flannelled shoulders, its jaws closing about his head. And then all was screaming and gunfire—which lit up the garage like the fourth of July and thundered, cracking, off its walls—as I piledrived Atticus and wrested the axe from him; as everyone scrambled for their weapons and the raptors pounced upon more Skidders.

"Lazaro!" I remember yelling—knowing his shotgun could blow the gate, knowing he'd opened locked doors with it before—before a man screamed nearby and I looked: and saw his attacker biting off the top of his head—just opening it like a watermelon, taking everything but his long, full beard.

And then there was a shotgun blast and we were falling back, still firing at the velociraptors, still firing into Atticus' men—lighting up everything and everyone as we ducked beneath the gate and burst into the rain. As we hustled down Marion Street with Roman thundering above us and the screams of the Skidders still echoing in our heads.

Toward the Exchange Building and a gutted triceratops in the window of a Starbucks. Toward the research and development lab of Roman's former employer ... and something we knew only as Gargantua.

Someone needed to say something, anything. The danger in silence was that, post-Flashback, one inevitably heard the emptiness, the melancholy: the sound of the world just breathing in and out, dreaming. So I said: "For her, the Flashback is over"—hoping it would break the spell of her liquefied eyes and deeply sunken sockets, the pale, wispy hair, the fuzzy white fungus in her nostrils and mouth. Hoping, I suppose, that it would drown out the Nothing—if only for a moment.

"No more power lunches for this babysan," said Lazaro, and spat. He kicked the spilt attaché case at the base of the cycad, where her feet should have been, and paper and cash swirled. "Here one minute—melded with a tree the next. Shit sucks."

Sam stepped closer, examining where the woman's face merged with the tree. "Initial Flashback, you think? Or an aftershock?"

I watched the rain—which had lessened to a drizzle— dribble down the corpse's face and neck. "I don't know, she seems pretty well preserved. Could have been an aftershock."

"Probably suffocated," said Nigel. "Tree manifested and her lungs couldn't expand. Jesus. What a horrible way to go."

I looked at Joan who was white as a ghost. "You all right?"

"Yeah. It's just that ..." She shook her head. "It's nothing."

She jumped as our walkie-talkies squawked; it sure looked like something to me. "Go ahead, Sea One," I said. "What's your twenty?"

I looked to see the Bell 206 arching over Elliott Bay.

"Just west of you—monitoring pack movements near the Colman ferry terminal. Carnotauruses, by the looks of it. I take it you're at the Exchange?"

"Affirmative—and awaiting instructions."

"Through the double doors, left at the first hall, all the way to the end. Austin Dynamics and Land Systems. They'll be a secure door—you'll have to blow it. And hurry, because there are predators of the human variety on the move in Pioneer Square."

I peered at the sky, at what Roman called the Mesozoic Borealis, watching the colors bleed in and out of each other, watching them shift and change shape. "Yeah, ah, about that. Requesting alternative escape route—Over. We have had contact with Skidders. I repeat, we have had contact with them. We—they're all dead. Over."

But there was nothing, just the sound of the helicopter.

At last Roman said, "That's unfortunate. But it doesn't change a thing. Escape route is still 1st Avenue through Pioneer Square to Edgar Martinez Drive—then I-90 to Issaquah. Do you copy?"

That's when I saw it: *him,* the kid, dirty-faced and wild-eyed, his hair like an unkempt mane, listening to us from the nearby stairwell—like the feral boy in *The Road Warrior,* I swear.

"Hey!" I shouted, drawing the attention of the others, "Hey, kid! Hold up!"

But he was already gone—climbing from the well at its opposite end, bolting up the shattered sidewalk like a gazelle. Weaving right at 2nd Avenue—where he vanished into the primordial mist.

"Jesus," said Lazaro, before the overheads had even finished flickering on. "I mean ... Who was this thing even built for, Godzilla?"

I stared at the vehicle, which was the length of a small yacht, say, 50 feet. "Well, not to put too fine a point on it, it was built for *us.* Or whoever survived whatever apocalypse Dannon had dreamed up."

I approached the rover and slid my hand up one of the tires—which was taller than I was, by about a foot. "Welcome to the world of big tech billionaires and their passion projects." The rubber felt stiff, unyielding, like polished wood. "His was to build a fully self-contained armored expedition vehicle—a kind of mini-Noah's Ark—something that could not only sustain life but go about exploring what was left of the world—if and when the shit ever hit the fan."

I circled the big rig while gazing up at its slanted cab and wide, black grill, its array of lights, its giant push and roll bars. The thing was like a van-version of the Cybertruck but on fucking steroids. "Reckon he was like Mr. Musk—in need of a challenge, but also a moral imperative to justify it. For him that was this apocalypse he saw coming." I paused to examine the roof turret and what appeared to be a .50-caliber machine gun. "A virus, maybe. Or a war. Dinosaurs probably weren't in his game plan."

"Looks they were getting ready to test it," said Sam. "Look."

I looked to where a massive steel ramp (we'd descended stairs to get to the production floor) ended at an equally massive door. "Good. Looks like this might be easier than we—"

There was a rattle of weapons followed by Lazaro shouting, "Stop! Get on the ground!" —and I hurried to see what the commotion was; at which instant I saw a man in a blue shop-coat standing by a huge sphere and holding what looked like a small, olive-colored ball over his head—a ball with a ring attached, through which he'd looped a trembling finger.

"He's got a bomb!" I shouted—but resisted raising my rifle. "Everyone just chill! Okay?"

No one did—chill, that is—but no one fired either, and a moment or two passed in silence.

At last the man said, "See this big tank here, this round monstrosity?" He indicated the white metal container next to him, which was taller even than he was. "That would be propylene gas—enough to level this entire floor, maybe the building itself. See this?" He nodded at the olive-colored ball. "That's your standard military-issue hand grenade, courtesy of the kids who were stationed here before they *and* the city fell. See those?" He nodded at some handles and hoses near the floor. "Those are the valves I loosened as you were making your way here. If you don't smell it yet, you will. It's strong. Now. Any questions?"

"Only one," I said, and pushed up my glasses. "What do you want?"

He shifted his footing as though preparing for a long standoff. "I want you to lower your weapons," he said, and wiggled his fingers near the pin— keeping himself on his toes. "Lower them and kick them toward me, all of you. Then we'll talk."

Nobody said anything.

At last I set down my rifle and motioned for the others to do the same. "Do it," I said, and slowly raised my arms. "You too, Lazaro. *Let's go.*"

The weapons clattered as they were placed on the floor and punted toward him.

He lowered his arms cautiously. "There, see? We're still capable of it—rational thought. It hasn't gone the way of the dinosaur." He laughed at that, but kept the grenade close to his chest. "Yet."

He looked at our weapons as though running calculations through his head. "There's Neanderthals roaming the streets, did you know that? Real ones—not supporters of President Tucker." He paused, seeming to size us all up. "Remember them? With their little red hats and faces all puffed in rage?" He chuckled. "Fell off the flat earth, I guess. No, these are genuine *Homo sapiens neanderthalensis*—right beside modern man and triceratops; right beside honkers from the Jurassic and Cretaceous and Triassic. Just sort of one big medley—like Time itself was put in a blender, or a concrete mixer, or a cream separator, and churned."

He seemed to relax a little and even lowered the grenade.

"I'm Ewan, by the way. Ewan Homes. I—I was *Gargantua's* chief engineer. Before life put us all in the blender."

"Jamie," I said. "Jamie Klein. This is Sam." I indicated the others. "That's Lazaro, Nigel, and Joan. We—we're from Issa—"

"Jamie, don't," interrupted Sam.

"It's all right," I said—and meant it. I trusted him; I don't know why. "We're from Issaquah. Got a camp there in what used to be a drive-in theater; it's got walls, vegetable gardens, some chickens and goats—there's even some generators, if you want to watch a movie. The thing is—Ewan—it's not overcrowded. And what I'm going to suggest just now is that—"

"Nothing leaves this facility," he snapped—simply, with finality. "That includes me." He raised the grenade tentatively and reached for the pin—then hesitated, his eyes searching mine, or seeming to. "No ... no, I don't hear it. It's not there." He lowered the olive-colored explosive slowly, tentatively. "The guile of the predator, the cunning of the fox. It's not there. You speak ... earnestly."

I let down my arms carefully, incrementally, maintaining eye contact. "I speak as someone who has sought *Gargantua* while not knowing it had a guardian, a sentinel, which is yourself, or at least how you see yourself. I speak as someone who has faced the Big Empty alone just as you have—and knows it is not for lack of bread that a man dies, but lack of purpose, and that you have found yours in the guarding of this machine, this vehicle—a vehicle that, for whatever reason, you cannot even drive yourself, or you would have done so already. And I'll offer you another way—Ewan, chief engineer at Austin Dynamics and Land Systems, whose budget was 8.5 million per fiscal year and who's assistant was named Roman Daystrom, your best friend—if you'll just turn off that fucking gas."

By the time I'd reintroduced Roman and Ewan via radio, and the former had convinced the latter to not only come with us but to let someone other than himself drive *Gargantua* (Ewan, we were told, was blind as a bat), and Nigel had escorted the engineer to his quarters so he could retrieve some of his effects, the clock on the wall of the shop read half past one—more than enough time for the Skidders to have organized some type of counter-strike; a fact that weighed heavily on my mind as the women and I began gathering up specs and schematics and Lazaro paced the room impatiently.

"What the hell's taking them so long? You heard Roman—carnotauruses, heading this way. Oh, I forgot. Nigel's on Jamaican Time."

"They have been gone awhile," said Sam. "Maybe we should—"

"It's no good splitting us up," I said. "There's no telling how quickly we might have to leave. Nigel's got it—everyone just chill." I looked at Lazaro. "Can you give us a hand with these? They're going to be heavy."

"Why the hell are we carting them along, then?" He snatched up one of the boxes with a huff and headed for *Gargantua.* "Or him, for that matter? Dude is definitely a few sandwiches short of a picnic."

"You going to fix this thing when it—" began Joan, but Lazaro was already up the ramp.

We continued working in silence.

At length Sam said, "Who was he, you think? That kid?"

I shrugged my shoulders. "Just a kid. Probably been on his own since the Flashback, who knows?" I heaped some manuals into a box—which created a cloud of dust. "He gave me a start, that's for sure. I didn't really get a good look at him."

"I did ..." She paused as though visualizing him. "He had bones around his neck, did you know that? Or teeth—like, really big ones. He'd strung them together as a sort of necklace. Isn't that odd, you think?"

Our faces were close as I stopped to reflect. "I don't know. Is it? Maybe he's extracting them from dead Barneys, like trophies. I confess, my first thought was that he'd gone feral. And yet ... He was wearing contemporary clothes, I remember that. Puffy coat, jeans, tennis shoes. I mean, he wasn't like Mowgli or anything."

She looked at me and started to grin. "I didn't think he was like *Mowgli* ..."

"All right! Drop your cocks and grab your socks," belted Lazaro—from the top of the ramp. "They're back."

I looked to see Nigel and Ewan entering the shop from the left, the latter seeming like an utterly new man—his hair no longer mussed; his clothes no longer a catastrophic mess.

"Apologies, apologies, a thousand apologies," he said, before pausing to admire *Gargantua.* "But a maiden voyage such as this requires a fresh change of clothes." He looked on a moment longer and then dropped to one knee—began ruffling through his overpacked bags. "Ah, yes, here it is. It's—I opened it with Nigel." He withdrew a corked bottle— which glinted darkly in the light from a high window. *"Voila!* One of eight bottles of Dom Perignon Rose champagne, Vintage 1959, served in Persepolis in 1971 by the then-Shaw of Iran."

He looked at us with a face flushed with excitement, and we looked back.

"To—to celebrate the 2500th anniversary of the founding of the Persian Empire ... by Cyrus the

Great." Disappointment stole over his face like a shadow. "It's—it's to break over the bow, as it were. To christen *Gargantua.*" Nobody said anything. "Yeah—well. Waste of liquor, anyway. Especially when I've got so much celebrating to do. I'll, ah—I'll just get the door. Over there."

He moved up the ramp toward the garage door.

That's when I thought of Lazaro's admonition, I don't know why: *You heard Roman—carnotauruses, heading this way.*

"Wait, Ewan," I said.

But he was already there, triggering the great door with his fist, turning to look at us as it rattled upward, pulling the cork from the champagne. "Life is for the living," he said, and toasted us with the bottle. "And this stuff ..." He poured champagne into his mouth and down the sides, soaking his clean, white shirt, splattering the floor with foam. "This is for howl—"

But then the door was open and they were there, the carnotauruses, and one closed its jaws about his scalp while another laid wide his abdomen (and another took up his legs) so that, howling, he was opened like a pizza being groped by eager hands. And then they themselves howled and piled over his body, and all we could do was to run—everyone save Nigel, who had his trimmer, which he started with a sputter—because our weapons were already in the rover.

Would we have made it to the truck if Nigel hadn't done what he did? I don't know—maybe. But I doubt it. The fact is these carnotauruses were *moving*—faster than I'd ever seen them move before—and had cut the distance between us in half before I heard the revving of Nigel's trimmer and saw him sweeping it across a dinosaur's belly, opening it like a can of spaghetti.

"Someone start the truck!" he shouted, his voice raw, animalistic, "I'll hold them off as long as I can!"

I scrambled up the stairs after Sam and Joan but before Lazaro. "Joan, this is your gig," I said, before essentially falling through a portal into the cockpit. "Get us out of here."

But she just stood there, looking around the deck and the crush of dials and switches; looking as if the vehicle itself might swallow her at any moment. "No ... No, I'm sorry. But I can't ... I just ..."

I indicated the co-pilot's seat. "Sam."

She buckled into her harness as I took the driver's seat and did the same, hoping that what Roman had told me was true—that *Gargantua* could pilot herself—and hoping, too, that I could remember the test protocol he'd so wisely insisted I study.

"Gargantua, this is Jamie—and I'm going to be your test driver today." I looked out the massive, slanted windshield to where Nigel had thrust his trimmer's saw-head into the mouth of a carnotaurus, only horizontally, after which he leveraged the shaft brutally—and popped off the top of the thing's head. "We are go for power on. I repeat: We are go for power on. Initiate protocol."

I watched as blood geysered from the beast's lower mandible—even as nothing seemed to happen with the vehicle.

"Gargantua. Initiate protocol."

"I got a bad feeling about this," said Sam, even as the creatures closed in around Nigel, and Lazaro opened fire from the ramp. "I mean, if you could just bounce in here and say 'go' then it obviously—"

"Clearance is Delta-Delta—*Dawn,*" I said rapidly, recalling the code words Roman had insisted I memorize, recalling how well he'd prepared me should something happen to Joan, as the consoles lit up like Christmas trees and the screens flickered to blue life; as the rover's hybrid engines hummed and whirred and pulsed, powerfully. "Issaquah via I-90, *go!*"

And then we were moving, smoothly, robustly (after an initial lurch), as one of the screens showed the stairs beginning to retract and Nigel rushed onto them—where he was assisted by Lazaro—as we clanked onto the ramp and powered up its traction-metal and finally burst onto the street.

"Sea One, this is Away Team Alpha, we are on our way!"

I looked up through the cockpit's huge windshield in time to see the Bell 206 thundering overhead—zooming toward Pioneer Square and the headquarters of the Skidders; zooming toward Edgar Martinez Drive and I-90 and *home.* "Do you copy?"

"Copy you loud and clear, Away Team Alpha," said Roman at last, euphorically, and laughed. "Congratulations."

I looked over my shoulder as Nigel and Lazaro joined us on the bridge, then forward again through the tinted windshield—where the streetlights were passing dangerously close to the roof. "Everybody hang on, we could run out of clearance fast."

There was a *frap-frap-frap* as the twigs of trees started colliding with us. That's when I first noticed it: him, her—a lone figure—walking out into the middle of the road, stopping between us and Pioneer Square. Turning to face us as I instinctively hit the brakes.

"Auto-pilot disengaged," said a voice—Majel Barrett's from *Star Trek,* I swear; some geek's idea of a joke.

"Is that who I think—" Sam started to say but then trailed off.

I peered through the angled glass, which was bullet-proof, I presumed, I mean it was *thick,* as the truck ground to a stop and the figure came into focus—beard, flannel, and all.

It was Atticus.

"Well, well," said Lazaro, sardonically. "Slippery motherfucker, isn't he?" He added: "What's that?"

I looked to where another figure had entered the street to join him, a smaller figure, wearing a puffy black coat and blue jeans, whose hair was wild and unkempt. A figure who wore a necklace of large teeth around his neck—T. rex teeth, by the looks of it—and smiled gap-toothed as Atticus ruffled his hair.

The kid. The feral boy. Mowgli, whatever.

But that wasn't all, for there were others now too—not Skidders, there were no beards or flannel or Converse shoes—just people: men, women and children, most of them disheveled, who walked out single-file and formed a living fence across the road— even as another group (visible on one of the monitors) did the same behind us. And it was at precisely that instant that I glimpsed the first of the red dots—which were fleeting, erratic, sometimes holding on a person's head, sometimes roaming— and realized just how much trouble we were in. How trapped we'd become.

Time had stopped—not because of any Flashback or roiling time-storm or strange, vague lights in the sky, or because fully three quarters of the human population had vanished without a trace (and been replaced with prehistoric flora and fauna), but because we'd been outsmarted, pure and simple. And now all we could do was watch, as the rows of people in front of us and behind began to lay themselves on the ground and another brought Atticus a megaphone—which he lifted to his mouth while steadying himself with his ax and directed at the rover's cab.

"Well, just check ... this ... out! Damn!" He acted as though he might slap his knees. *"Gargantua One.'* What do you know? I mean, what will they think of next?"

The feral kid appeared to laugh as the wind gusted suddenly and the branches of the trees swayed.

"Those are *some* prenatal vitamins, I must say. I can see now why you thought this was important enough to risk your lives. Not to mention kill or allowed to be killed some of my best men."

My mind raced. Time. We needed time. I searched the banks of switches and readouts for a means of communication and found a toggle marked 'loudspeaker,' which I flipped.

"I seem to recall you were about to chop off Sam's head," I said, hoping it would keep him jabbering for at least a minute.

"And snip such a fine tassel?" He laughed. "Not on this watch, Midtown. You need to learn to recognize bullshit when you see it—"

I switched off the loudspeaker. "We need ideas—fast."

"For what?" said Nigel. "You can see all the red dots. He's got us in a hopeless situation, tactically."

"That's *bullshit,* man," snapped Lazaro. "There's a machine gun on top of this thing."

"And what are you going to shoot at? The air? They're hidden in the buildings all around. You'll be lucky to get in a burst before—"

"He's right," I said. "It's no good. Those people aren't just human barriers—they're hostages. We start fooling around with that gun ... and they're toast." I keyed the mic of my radio. "Sea One, this is Away Team Alpha. Come back."

Atticus continued: "... gangland theatrics. How else was I going to get you to talk? I knew you were after *some* kind of kale ..."

Our radios squawked. "Go ahead."

"Listen, Roman, quickly: We are surrounded by Skidders and need technical data regarding

Gargantua— defense mechanisms, weapons systems, whatever you got. And we need it fast."

He responded almost instantly. "Where is Ewan, *asleep?*"

I started to speak but hesitated, wondering if I should tell him now or later; if I should disrupt his focus. "He ... he's passed out in the back. He was ... he was pretty drunk."

But there was no response and we listened to Atticus as we waited; luckily for us, the motherfucker liked to talk.

"... and consider yourselves lucky you didn't run into, say, Antifa. Don't laugh—those little fuckers are hard. Like a bunch of Viet Cong running around in black pajamas. Saw them go up against a militia once—might have been White Out, I'm not sure ..."

"Okay, listen up," came Roman at last, his voice full of urgency. "The gun up top can be operated from inside as well as out, you just have to use the joystick, which is on the right side of the driver's seat. There should be a pair of sighting goggles also, hanging above, which are slaved to the .50-cal—you'll use these to acquire targets. Just hit 'auto' on the joystick and you'll be golden. There's also smoke dispensers mounted on both sides of the vehicle, the switch is right above you, but I don't advise using them—they're too effective and you'll be blinded for several minutes. At least. Other than that the vehicle was designed primarily for exploration, so I don't know what—can I provide any sort of air cover? Prop-wash, for example?"

"Negative, I repeat, negative. It's too tight in here. Just stand by."

Atticus, meanwhile, was still going on: "... ever seen a pack of allosaurs take down a diplodocus? That's what this was like. Just hit and run, hit and run, until the big dumb bastards collapsed from their own weight. Now they're dead—and a bunch of skinny anarchists have AR-15s ..."

I peered at the old buildings through the trees and at the darkened windows, many of them without glass. If it had been even slightly foggy or misty—as it had been earlier—we might have traced the beams right back—

My heart must have skipped a beat, I'm sure of it. *Jesus,* I thought. *Could it be that simple?*

"What is it?" asked Sam, sounding concerned.

I reached for the goggles and slowly slid them on, then gripped the joystick cautiously. "See that switch right there? The illuminated blue one?" She nodded warily, her face pale. "That's the smoke dispensers. When I give the word I want you to flip it, okay? Don't be scared."

"What are you doing?" snapped Lazaro, with a clear edge to his voice. "Sandahl, what is he doing?"

"I'm getting ready to target those snipers," I said, and pressed the 'auto' switch, making sure to keep my head perfectly still lest the machine gun swivel and alert Atticus. "Nigel, get ready on the loudspeaker. On my word only I want you to order those people to get up and get clear. Make sure they understand—we are coming through. There can be no confusion. Lazaro, I want you to open the side door—but do not lower the ramp—and take a position; at my word you'll use my M4 to clear targets on the *right* side of the truck only, understand? I'll take care of the left and then swing around to help you."

I waited for him to acknowledge and when he didn't I snapped, "Do you understand? We don't have time for this."

"Yes, I understand!"

"Good. Now—Joan. Where are you, girl?"

She stirred in the seat behind me. "I'm—I'm sorry, Jaime. I'm so sorry. But I—"

"You don't have to be," I said. "I know it's cramped in here. And I'm sorry I didn't listen to you when you tried to tell me about ... your condition. But you're going to make it, all right? We all are. Just buckle up and hold tight, and try to focus on what's outside. Just like you did in the helicopter— okay? You got this."

"I got this," she repeated, and exhaled sharply.

Atticus, meanwhile, had been counting down. "Three ... two ... *one.*" He sighed and lowered the megaphone—then lifted it to his mouth again. "The problem with you, Jaime, is that you just—don't—listen. Now I just explained to you what was going to happen if I reached 'one' and you hadn't come out, and *goddamned* if you didn't come out. So. What's going to happen now is that we're going to kill one of these people for every 30 seconds you remain inside the vehicle—starting immediately." He directed the bullhorn at the upper floors of one of the buildings. "Hershel? You awake up there?"

"Get ready," I said.

"I'm awake," came a voice, though it was impossible to tell exactly where from.

"Fine," said Atticus. "Hershel, in 30 seconds, I want you to place your site on the head of ... that little girl, right there." He gestured at a storefront on our right side—Simply Seattle. "Green coat, last one on the end, right next to the display window. Copy that there, Chief?"

The man didn't hesitate. "Twenty-nine! 28! 27 ..."

I toggled the loudspeaker myself. "We're coming out," I said, suddenly, and glanced at Sam. "We're trying to figure out how."

There was a silence as Atticus seemed to think about this.

At last he said, "Well, how complicated could it be? Just open the door. Hershel, keep counting ..."

"Twenty-three, 22, 21 ..."

"It's not that simple," I hurried to say, "It's, like, pressurized or something." To the others I said, "On my mark, okay? Get ready."

"We're at 18 seconds and counting, James," said Atticus. "Best clean your glasses and get with it."

"Seventeen, 16, 15 ..."

"Okay! Okay. We're depressurizing. Right ... *now.*"

And then Sam was toggling the smoke as I gripped the joystick tightly and Nigel took over the loudspeaker and Lazaro opened the side door, after which we cursed loudly and bent to our tasks, and, together, threw wide the gates of Hell.

It started, innocuously enough, with the *thump, thump, thump* of the smoke grenades, which launched at an angle from both sides of the cab and bounced off the overhanging tree branches—as well as breaking at least one nearby window—before falling to the pavement and bursting into clouds of gray smoke. Nor did anything happen immediately— almost as if everyone outside were in a state of shock. But then the smoke began to rise, obscuring everything, and illuminating too the beams of the lasers—which lengthened as I tracked them and led straight to the top floors of Doc Maynard's Public House—at which I depressed the 'fire' button and lit them up; even as Lazaro opened fire on the other side and feedback whined from the loudspeakers.

"Move—if you would live," shouted Nigel. "Get up and run, all of you! We're advancing."

But we'd spent our surprise and what Skidders remained in the windows rallied, opening fire indiscriminately, shooting blindly into the smoke, as their muzzles flashed like Xs and we continued to cut them down; as Nigel repeated his directive and my foot hovered over the gas. "Are they clear yet, Sam? Are they out of the way?"

I continued to fire even as bullets impacted against the windshield and side window, cracking them in rings, leaving huge craters.

"I don't know, I think so," she said. "They're scrambling, I saw that much."

"Then we're going," I said. "Nigel, give them a final warning."

"But how can you drive with the windows smashed?" protested Sam—even as more rounds impacted the glass. "How can—"

"Engage the auto-pilot!" I shouted, aiming at what appeared to be the last holdout, holding down the 'fire' button, feeling the cab vibrate and shake.

"But I don't know—"

"Got it," blurted Joan—having rallied herself, or so it seemed.

And then the engines were humming, pulsing—winding up like great turbines, moving us forward into the mists.

"We're all clear!" shouted Lazaro. "It's Issaquah or bust!"

And with that we emerged from the clouds; to see what could only be Atticus himself running down 1st Avenue, his unbuttoned flannel shirt flying out behind him, his Converse sneakers pounding the pavement. The feral kid, meanwhile, was nowhere to be seen.

"Jesus, does he even know we're coming?" asked Sam.

"No," I said, squinting between the cracks. "We're on electric."

"Good," said Lazaro. "Run the fucker over."

I tapped the gas pedal, to take it out of auto-pilot, having found a spot through which I could see clearly. "I'm reverting to manual," I said, having no intention of running him down like a dog.

But nothing seemed to happen; we just continued moving forward—picking up speed—until trees were blowing past on one side and buildings were blurring past on the other.

"It'll go around," said Joan. "The sensors haven't picked him up yet, that's all."

But I wasn't so sure as the gap between us closed rapidly—so rapidly I could see his buttocks pumping beneath the skinny jeans and his keys dancing wildly at his hip. And then he disappeared beneath the rig with a pronounced *thump* and the cab jolted, bouncing once, and I glanced at the rear-view monitor in time to see a skid of dark blood and bone and guts extending out behind us almost indefinitely.

"Okay ... so I thought I was better," said Joan, still staring at the screen—her face green as a ghost. "But I'm not." Her cheeks puffed suddenly as though she might vomit. "We need to pull over, I think. Like, *now.*"

"Okay. I'll try," I said, and tapped the gas pedal.

But this time, control reverted back to me—as it was supposed to do—and as we passed Jackson Street I began looking for a place to pull over, because it was finished, I knew. We were safe.

We'd survived the Dinosaur Apocalypse. Again.

By the time we did pull over—or rather, ground to a halt in the middle of the street—rain was starting to speckle the windshield (or what was left of it) and the sky had darkened, none of which prevented Joan from leaping onto her seat the moment we stopped and grabbing the handle of one of the ceiling hatches.

"Is that a good idea?" I asked, as she turned the handle and pushed the hatch open. "We haven't even had a look around yet—"

But she had already burst through the opening and was gasping for air, sucking it into her lungs in great, shuddering gulps, exhaling as though she'd been holding her breath for a lifetime. "I—I don't care," she rasped, as though she were collapsing from exhaustion. "Couldn't ... couldn't breathe. Couldn't—do it a second longer."

"What's wrong with her?" asked Lazaro.

"She's fine," I said, breathing in the fresh air myself, feeling relieved, almost euphoric. "Little bit of claustrophobia, that's all. Take all the time you need, Joan. We're done with this now. We're all done."

Everybody seemed to relax in their seats, exhaling, stretching their muscles. It was the first real rest we'd had since leaving the drive-in that morning.

"Well, would you look at that," said Lazaro at last, peering out his window, and laughed.

I followed his gaze to where a black awning with white letters read COWGIRLS INC – AMERICAN SALOON.

"Never heard of it," I said, and winked at Sam.

"I could go for a drink or five about now," said Joan, and laid her head on her arms.

"I could go for one of those waitresses dancing on the bar and shaking her ass in my face," said Lazaro.

"Ewan had the right idea," sighed Joan, and shifted her weight. "With that bottle of champagne, I mean." She fell silent for a moment as though remembering. "What was he saying when ... when ..."

I thought back on it, on that awful moment when the carnotauruses had torn him limb from limb. "He was in the middle of saying 'howl,' I think," I said, and slumped against my window. "That the champagne was for howling, not busting over *Gargantua,* to christen it. I think he'd been alone so long that he'd died a little, or even a lot. We'd given him hope. A reason to howl at the moon, or something."

Nobody said anything as the clouds rumbled overhead and the rain grew heavier, drizzling around the ringed cracks in the windshield, trickling down Joan's coveralls.

"I want to dance in the rain," said Sam, softly.

"We want you to too," said Lazaro.

"Aaoooh!" crooned Joan, and when I looked she'd stood straight again and spread her arms at the sky.

"Aaoooh!" responded Lazaro, almost as though he were drunk.

And then Nigel joined in, followed by Sam, and finally myself, and there we all were, howling at the sky like a bunch of damn lunatics, beating our chests for having survived another day—spreading our fiery, Phoenix wings in defiance of what we'd done and still had to do and what had become of the world.

And it was on the tip of my tongue to suggest we actually go in and have a drink—or five—when Joan's body seized up like a vice and her voice became muffled, at which I squinted through Lazaro's window and saw the lower body of the tyrannosaur (or whatever it was), and realized its head would have been exactly where she was—and that the new sound I was hearing, which was a garbled sound, an obscene sound, was that of Joan screaming; whimpering; suffocating no doubt in the monstrous animal's palette, before it jerked its head and she was yanked clean from the hatch. Before the great and terrible animal stepped back and began shaking her like a ragdoll, even though she was surely dead already, hurling her against the pavement with a sickening *smack,* pinning her there with its tri-clawed foot; which is when I stepped on the gas—but not before seeing her come apart like mozzarella—and drove away as fast as I could.

After which we drove the rest of the way home
in silence and tried not to think of all the blood
splattered around the hatch and pooled like thick,
dark wine in her seat. After which we kept our heads
down and our eyes alert, all the way to Issaquah and
the drive-in we called home. All the way until we
greeted Roman at the heli-pad with open arms and
walked together, through the cool shadows of the
carports, to our respective campers and trailers and
RVs.

THE DREAMING CITY

We would have been quite the sight had there been anyone left alive to see us, rumbling up N. La Brea Avenue in *Gargantua One*—we'd disengaged the electric motor and were running the 16.1-liter diesel only, but that's another story—the expedition vehicle's stainless steel hull glinting back at us from the shop windows and its parabolic antenna whirling; its great pistons rattling.

"Rollin' down—the Imperial Highway, with a big, nasty redhead at my side," Sam sang along with the stereo. "Santa Ana winds blowin' hot from the north, and we were *born to ride ...*"

"Jesus, not again," moaned Lazaro. He reached past her toward the deck but she batted his hand away.

Nigel, meanwhile, had to shout over the music: "You want to follow La Brea all the way to Hollywood Boulevard—then hang a right. We're looking for *Gower Street.*"

"Looks like it's going to be smooth sailing," said Sam.

I glanced out the side window as we passed Pink's Hot Dogs—the awning of which was covered with moss and vines—saw startled Compies scatter like mice. "Let's hope Roman's mission is going as well."

Black Mr. Fantastic—please; he'd nicknamed himself—was skeptical. "At a big base like Lewis-McChord? I doubt it. That place is one big Army surplus store now. You really think he's going to just waltz in there and fly out with an Apache?"

"Hard to say," I drawled. "But I do know this: If he succeeds, and if we're successful in securing Eagleton's bunker, nothing will be able to touch us again. That is, if it's still, how shall I say it? *Available.*"

"It will be," said Nigel. "Because nobody knows it's there."

"Except *you,*" sneered Lazaro. "His former lawn guy. Isn't that it?"

"Ya, mon—that's right. I told you: he showed it to us while we were working. Just rolled up in his 1947 Packard one day and started jabbering like we were best friends. Nice guy—sharp as a whip. I knew it was him right away because I'd seen him on *The Tonight Show;* and because he was wearing those same tinted glasses he likes so much."

"Well, what if he's there?" asked Sam.

"He won't be. He never actually lived there, as I said. It was just one of his passion projects—like this rover was for Steve Dannon." He fell quiet as though in deep thought. "Ain't it a shame. All those luxuries—the swimming pool, the indoor park, the gourmet galley—not to mention the food stores and hydroponics—all of it just sitting there, collecting dust. Meanwhile, there's people living in cardboard boxes."

"Or was," said Sam.

"Yeah, but, he *gave,* too. Like, a lot," I said. "I went to college on one of his scholarships. Read him all the time when I was younger—he was kind of a hero to me. Never thought I'd be barnstorming one of his homes."

"You never thought you'd be running from dinosaurs, either," said Sam. She reached over and wiggled my cheek—roughly. "And now look at you go."

"Okay, here it is," said Nigel. "Take a right."

I took a right—swinging the giant rig onto Hollywood Boulevard, watching the big streetlights pass absurdly close to the windshield. "It won't be long. We're going to want to—"

"Whoa, whoa, whoa," said Mr. Fantastic, having noticed the thing—its startling blue, its clean, perfect white—even before I did. "Slow, slow, slow. Go back."

I left off the gas and applied the brakes—which hissed and squealed, like scythes—bringing us to a complete stop. Then I backed up—the different torque causing the gears to rap and wind—until we had drawn alongside the banner and the cycad trees supporting it.

At last Sam said: "Okay, Batman, riddle me this. What's stranger than a Donald J. Tucker banner in the middle of L.A.?" She turned to face Mr. Fantastic.

We all turned to face him—our very own Reed Richards; the Nutty Professor to our Desert Isle. Our Dr. Zarkov.

"How about a Donald J. Tucker banner that was put here recently; as in, after the Flashback," he said—and nodded at the trees. "Because those are cycads—bennettitales, to be precise, from the Upper Jurassic—*not* palms. And what *that* means, kids, is— we're not alone."

We drove on in silence, Sam having killed the music (*The Best of Randy Newman,* as I recall), past the TCL Chinese Theatre—where a pack of raptors were picking over the corpse of a diplodocus calf—past the Capitol Records Building (whose round, spired roof was crowded with seagulls and pterodactyls), then left on N. Gower Street and up to Scenic Avenue— which would take us to Beachwood Drive and on to the Hollywoodland hills. That is, had its shoulders not been choked with cycads and its roadway blocked by a black allosaurus (we were all pretty much experts on dinosaurs now): which had simply lazed over in the middle of the asphalt as though it were sunning itself—its long, sinewy legs stretched luxuriously and its tail straight and unfurled, its great, blood-red crests glistening.

"Oh, for fuck's sake," I said—and brought us to a gradual halt.

I honked the horn—taking note of the dead triceratops in the reeds (which was partially eaten), as well as the allosaur's obviously full belly—but there was no response.

"Just go, man," said Lazaro. "It'll move. And if it doesn't, so what."

"He's right, Jamie," said Sam. "I don't think we have time for this."

I put it in gear and inched forward—revving the engine even as I laid on the horn, moving to within a few feet of it.

Still it did not move—only twitched a little as though it were dreaming; maybe flicked its tail once slightly.

"Jesus, are you kidding me?" I was beginning to lose my patience. "Let's go! It's time to pick 'em up and move 'em out."

I inched still closer—until one of the thing's outstretched feet vanished beneath what passed for the hood. Then it *did* move, rearing its head and gnawing at the push bar—only gently, playfully, like a cat disrupted from a nap—before getting up suddenly and shuffling aside; at which I stepped on the gas and we lurched forward—turning wide as we passed through the intersection; rumbling up Beachwood like an out-of-control freight train; breaking off heavy branches like twigs.

I looked into my sideview mirror even as Sam did the same, saw the thing bounding after us like a leopard, like a wraith, gaining rapidly.

"What is it?" snapped Mr. Fantastic. "What's going on?"

I glanced between it and the road, accelerating rapidly. "It's chasing us. *Fuck.* Better get up into the Crow's Nest, Lazaro. Just don't get trigger-happy; we're gonna need the ammo. Nigel, I'm going to need you to—"

"It'd be best to just let it go," said Mr. Fantastic. "I mean, what's it going to do—bite through solid steel?" He put a hand on my shoulder, comfortingly, reassuringly. "Save the ammo, Jamie. It'll give up before we get there."

I looked around the cockpit: at the banks and banks of instrumentation, the suffocating array of dials and switches—before focusing on a glowing blue toggle; and flipped it. "I don't know about you, Doctor ..." There was a *thump-thump-thump* as I turned to face him. "But where I'm from—they call that 'borrowing trouble.'"

And then the smoke grenades had detonated and we were crashing through their clouds—at which

I hit the brakes hard and hung an immediate left, skidding onto a side street, and whereupon we quickly circumnavigated the block to burst back onto Beachwood. Where we instantly realized—just before swinging north—that we could no longer see the street south of us; nor, for that matter, any evidence whatsoever of a pursuing allosaurus—black with red crests or otherwise.

I'd be lying if I said I hadn't already felt uneasy—even before we rounded the bend and saw the big pickups. Deronda Drive was that kind of road: the kind that started normally but then began to twist and turn, and to narrow, climbing all the while, so that the houses on both sides (some nearly palatial while others seemed little more than glorified hippie shacks) closed in all around us. Add to that the fact that we'd run out of places to turn back, and you can imagine how on edge we (already) were when we saw the crashed gate and the occupied vehicles beyond it.

Nor had those occupants taken long to train weapons on us—about 4 seconds, by my count—snapping them out through side windows and an open door even as the men in the payloads (one of which was equipped with a large-caliber machine gun and the other some type of rocket launcher) did the same.

And then there we were, faced off like the Hatfields and the McCoys—only we weren't ready—there beneath the sun in the Hollywoodland hills with the Santa Ana wind blowing and *Gargantua* idling and their blue and white Tucker flags fluttering, proclaiming "Keep America Great" and "No More Bullshit." As though there was still somehow a recognizable government—a recognizable *enemy;* something they could project all their fear and loathing and frustration onto, just as before. As though nothing had changed since the Flashback at all.

I reached up for the targeting goggles slowly, knowing the new windows were tinted but not wanting to take any chances, but didn't put them on. "Nobody get excited," I said. "It's just ... it's just a precaution."

"Oh, Jesus," whispered Sam.

"No, he's right," said Mr. Fantastic. "Because—see that rocket launcher?" He pointed at the truck furthest back—a black Dodge Ram with pig ear exhaust stacks and a custom lift. "That, my friends, is what you call bad news. Now, I don't pretend to know what that is, exactly, but what it reminds me of is the French MILAN ..." He got out of his seat and crouched in front of the windshield. "Okay. Yuh. See that dome just inside the barrel? That's the warhead. Big, right? Nasty, right? That's because it's an *anti-tank* weapon." He looked at Sam suddenly—to make his point, I guess. "It *kills* tanks, see. Stops them dead in their tracks. They've even been confirmed to have taken out a U.S.-supplied Abrams—that's the main battle tank of the U.S. Army—in Iraq, in 2017, during their conflict with the Kurds."

He turned to me before making eye contact with each and every one of us. "And you better believe it when I say, people, that that thing will cut through this hull like it's tinfoil. So Jamie's doing the right thing; providing he keeps his focus on that missile launcher. The question is, do we shoot first and eliminate the threat preemptively—by taking out the operator and anyone else who dares to go near it—or do we try to talk to them? Reason with them? Convince them we're not a threat?"

"But we are a threat," said Sam—softly, gravely. "We're here for the bunker. And so are they, obviously. Or they've seized it already. I mean, look at what we're driving. There's a machine gun on the roof, for—"

"I say we shoot first," interjected Nigel—after which he seemed shocked that he'd actually said it. "She's right, I mean—S-sandahl. Sam. We are a threat; and there's no point in trying to deny it. So are they. I mean, come on. You *saw* the banner. If that's not a territorial claim, I don't know what is.

And they're white trash, anyway, mon. Stupid and dangerous on—"

"Yo, pound sand!" snapped Lazaro. "I voted for Tucker, too, you know, and I'm not some crazed redneck you can just ..." He trailed off suddenly and looked around—as if for approval—but nobody said a word.

"—on the face of it," finished Nigel, succinctly. He looked at Mr. Fantastic and then at me. "And you know it as well as I do."

I looked out through the long, narrow windshield: at the armed, thickset men—most of them were at last partially overweight—and their dirty, dark-colored trucks; at the poised rifles and trained, glinting machine gun, the rocket launcher with its big, tank-killing warhead.

Mr. Fantastic, meanwhile, had gotten back into his seat. "What's it going to be, Jamie?"

I unbuckled my harness and leaned forward, elbows on my knees—began rubbing my temples.

At last I said, "And this is the only way in? The only road that can be used?"

Paper rattled as Nigel shifted. "Mount Lee Drive, that's right. Winds all the way up to the City of Los Angeles Communications Facility, which is right above the Hollywood sign."

"And beneath it? The sign, I mean? *That's* our bunker?"

"About 50 yards down from it, that's right. Only accessible by air or on foot from there, since the private road from below was removed."

I peered out at the trucks, which shimmered in the heat. "How in the hell did they find out? That's what I want to know."

"Does it matter?" asked Mr. Fantastic. "Besides; we don't actually *know* that they have—we don't know anything, really. Not why or how long they've been here, nor how many of them there are, we don't even know if—"

"That's bullshit, mon. We know it's a train because that's how they roll; and we know there's more of them—probably up there rooting around because they've never actually been here and don't know what they're looking for. No, scratch that—they're probably on their way *here,* because these assholes have already radioed them while we sit here and have a goddamn debate about—"

"Nigel."

"About—"

"*Nigel.* Shut the fuck up."

"But ..."

"Here." I handed the targeting goggles back to him. "Put them on. *Shut the fuck up.* And put them on."

"Wait, what?" Lazaro just glared at me; it was almost as though I'd stabbed his mother. "Is this a joke?"

"I know, you're checked out on the internal gun control. But let's be honest, Dwayne. You don't want to hurt these people. Hell, they're like family, right?" I clapped him on the shoulder briskly. "Just one, big, happy Tucker Train. One big tent from Cabela's. Isn't that right?"

"What the hell are you talking about?"

"Sam, get the ramp," I instructed, and watched as she flipped the toggle—reluctantly.

"Because we're going to go meet your friends with our hands up," I said. "And you, sir, are going to do all the talking."

"Ready?"

I looked at Lazaro and he looked back. "Ready." He squinted at me suddenly. "Why wouldn't I be?"

I shrugged. "No reason." I took a deep breath. "Okay. Remember, hands in the air."

He put his hands in the air.

Then we moved out; stepping into the sunshine from the cool shadow of the expedition vehicle, raising our hands as though we were surrendering.

"Easy does it ..."

There was a rattle of arms as they noticed us and hurriedly re-trained their weapons.

"Halt! Who goes there?"

Both of us froze. "A-Americans. Two of us," said Lazaro. "We want to talk."

The wind blew; the sun beat down. Nobody said anything.

"Daryl," snapped one of them at last—after which a skinny blonde dude stepped out (he couldn't have been more than 17) and seemed to hesitate; looking at us over his rifle, shifting his weight from one foot to the other, before shuffling forward quickly and giving us a pat-down—briefly, hurriedly. "They're good," he said.

The man who'd directed him to frisk us—he looked like John Goodman, I swear—motioned for us to come forward.

"That's close enough," he said, after we'd closed the gap. "Trent, Brady, Mitchell—cover us. Everyone else, hold your positions." He seemed to relax—slowly, grudgingly. "Americans, you say." He handed the skinny guy his weapon—some kind of long rifle, who knows. "That doesn't really feel complete to me. You say you're Americans. Which one?"

Lazaro and I glanced at each other.

"Both of us," said Lazaro, and straightened a little. "Born and bred."

Jesus, I thought, and rubbed my brow.

The man stiffened. "Hands in the air."

I raised my hands—after which he seemed to lighten, and just chuckled. "No, I mean: *Which America?*"

I looked at Lazaro, who hesitated. "The—the only one," he said. "The only America. Tucker's America." He feigned confusion. "What other is there? I mean; since the Flashback, that is?"

The man didn't say anything, only glanced at the skinny kid, whose face was a wreck of pimples.

That's when we heard it: the sound of diesel engines—lots of them—coming down the hill, coming down Mount Lee Drive.

He snatched the radio from his belt. "We're over here—in front of the trucks. We've got two of them," he said.

And then the trucks began to appear, rumbling down the service road like a cavalry, like an armored support column, black smoke billowing from their exhaust stacks and Tucker flags flying; their huge, aggressive-looking front grills gleaming, the radio and C.B. antennas whipping—until they'd made a parking lot of the base of the hill and their drivers had begun getting out—many of them wearing red hats and loud shirts, campaign buttons, red, white and blue leis—and all of whom headed our way and partially surrounded us; at least, until a singular personage—a towering man in blue jeans and a black T-shirt, who wore a strikingly-sculpted beard and a gleaming white Stetson—parted them like the Red Sea: the **MAGA** Nephilim, the "No More Bullshit" Moses, and joined our little drum circle.

"They say they want to talk," said the first man, "but I wanted to wait until you got here. We, ah, we don't know anything yet."

The man in the Stetson just looked at us, his hands on his hips. Then he took a few steps toward *Gargantua* and paused, his great, broad back facing us.

His silence seemed to make the first man uncomfortable. "What do you think? You, ah, ever seen anything like it?"

The towering figure didn't move, didn't budge, only continued staring at the stainless steel vehicle, which gleamed beneath the sun.

At length he said: "Devin tells me you want to talk." He paused to clear his throat. "That you—that you got something to say." He reached up slowly and stroked his beard—thoughtfully, meditatively—before turning to face us. "So say it. *Talk.* You can start with your names. I'm Denton."

We both just looked at him, unsure how to begin.

"I'm Jamie," I said, and held out my hand. "Jamie Klein. This here is Lazaro."

He looked at my hand as though he was uncertain what to make of it. Then he gripped it; gently at first, but then squeezing suddenly and briefly, crushingly—if only for an eyeblink. *Message received,* I thought.

He shook hands with Lazaro.

I chose not to waste any time: "We're here for one of the parabolic antennas," I lied. "From the Communications Facility. Our engineer thinks he can use it to replace our existing one, which is malfunctioning."

Denton raised an eyebrow—as though that wasn't what he'd expected. He glanced at *Gargantua* and then back to me. "For that?"

I nodded, saying nothing.

"I see," he said. He raised his chin abruptly. "So you're not—affiliated with anyone? FEMA? Red Cross? The United Nations?"

I shook my head.

"NATO? EUFOR?" He looked us up and down, first me, then Lazaro. "No. I don't suppose you are." He indicated *Gargantua* again. "And the rig?"

I told him the truth: that someone in our group had known about it before the Flashback, in Seattle, and that after the time-storm we'd stolen it. And that that was all—

"Seattle?" exclaimed the first man, 'Devin,' incredulously. He harrumphed. "I thought you said you were *Americans.*"

Denton suppressed a smirk. His eyes had lit up at mention of Seattle too. "That where you're from, Jamie Klein?"

I could see where this was going. "Originally—yes. But we left the shithole to seek a warmer climate, a *southern* climate." I looked him directly in the eye. "And better people. Loyal people. Like you." I looked around at the others. "Like *all* of you."

He followed my gaze, seeming to appreciate the sentiment (although it was hard to tell, really, because he was squirrely, this Denton: a sidewinder dressed as a straight-shooter). "Well, I'm glad you feel that way, Jamie. I really am. But we've got a problem—several of them, actually. The first is, we can't let you do that: take the antenna. As part of the Array, it's got to go—it's got to be destroyed. Second, we're not currently accepting—which is to say, if you're looking to join our train, we can't take you. And the third is—we've already claimed this land. Hollywood, that is. Everything from Beverly Hills in the south to the Santa Monica foothills in the north—it's, ah, it's ours now. I'm thinking you probably noticed our banners. Oh, yeah. And the fourth." His blue eyes met my own, piercingly, unflinchingly.

"You're trespassing. And you need to leave. Like, now. Also—if we see you again," He shrugged, real cute-like: "We'll execute you."

I looked from him to Devin and onto the pimply kid. "So that's it. No discussion, no compromise; not even a reason why."

"There's a reason. It's because there's important work that needs to be done." He half-turned to face the others. "Isn't that so? Isn't there important work to be done?"

"Important work," said a woman in a foam campaign hat, and smiled. *"American* work."

"To end the Chinese Flashback," said someone else.

"And detonate the charges," said another. "To knock down the Array."

I must have looked confused. "I—Okay. What's the Array?"

He raised an eyebrow sharply. "You mean you don't know?" He looked from me to Lazaro. "Neither of you?"

"Yeah, I know," said Lazaro. "It—it's a secret high-power, high-frequency transmitter ... said to be somewhere in the U.S." He looked at his shoes as though vaguely ashamed. "Some say it's Chinese. Others say deep state. You know ... conspiracy stuff."

Denton just looked at him. "Conspiracy stuff," he said. He began pacing around us. "Well, let me tell you—Lazaro from Seattle—we've been up there, to this so-called 'Communications Facility,' and there ain't nothing normal about it; all right? Fact is, it's been *designed* to look like just another antenna farm, that's how it's stayed hidden all these years. Another fact is: it's home to the second High-frequency Active Auroral Research Program, or HAARP[2], which just happens to be what caused the Flashback."

He circled back around to face us and paused. "Got it? That's what started it all, see. That's what brought hell down upon us." When neither of us said anything, he added, *"They were messing with the ionosphere, man, don't you get it?* That's what let Them in ..." He indicated the lights in the sky, which hadn't been particularly active since we'd left Seattle. "That's when They became aware of us. When They—how did H.G. Wells say it? 'Drew their plans against us.'"

Everyone seemed to look at me, I have no idea why.

"You're fucking crazy," I said. "You—you've totally lost it."

"Have I?"

"It's a fucking *antenna farm,* Denton!" I glanced around us at the throngs of people. "I mean, is that what you people actually *believe?* Christ, did it steal the election, too? Is that what kind of bullshit you're trying to pass off?" I glared at Denton. "We're done here. Let's go, Lazaro."

"Now wait just a fucking—"

And he lunged at me—which was followed by the sound of *Gargantua's* .50 caliber swinging around, locking into position. Which was followed by it ratcheting down, down, until it was trained on Denton alone.

"Nobody move!" he shouted, splaying his hands, even as there was a riot of shifting arms. "Is that clear?"

But nobody did; move, that is, not even when Lazaro and I walked back the way we had come and ascended the ramp into *Gargantua;* where I gave the order to retreat and go back down the hill and Sam did, operating the rover like a champ—even though she'd only driven it twice before—backing into a driveway (one I hadn't even noticed) to reverse direction, taking us all the way to Rodgerton Street and beyond.

"Wait, *that's* Hollywood Park?"

I looked out the windshield as Sam pulled over on Canyon Lake Drive and killed the engine, which dieseled and rattled, briefly. "It's a park, what did you expect?"

Lazaro cupped his eyes, peering out the side window. "I don't know. Like, a statue of Marilyn Monroe, or somethin'. You know, with the wind all up in her shit and—"

"That's Palm Springs," said Nigel. "'Forever Marilyn,' on Museum Way. You'd like it."

"How the fuck would you know what I'd like?"

"It's an up-skirt. Just your speed."

"Hey, *fuck you, Jamaica.* Why don't you just—"

"Alright, knock it off, both of you," I said. "Nigel, let's have a look at that map."

We all gathered around as Nigel spread it between himself and Sam.

"I'm afraid it hasn't changed much," he said. "There's still no road other than Mount Lee Drive. And you saw the terrain; Gargantua can't handle that."

"What about on foot?" I circled a tangle of residential roads with my finger. "So we know these are blocked; what if we headed northeast straight from the park and just circumnavigated the whole mess?"

"Could work, but it would take time, and we don't know what's in those—"

"Hills, precisely," interjected Mr. Fantastic. "Look, see these? All these peaks and valleys? It's like a great big washboard, right? Well, see, that's precisely the kind of terrain welterweights like Utahraptor and Phorusrhacos love, because it allows them to herd prey into the lowlands and trap it there."

He looked at me gravely, solemnly. "In other words, we'd be walking straight into a kill box."

I sat back in my seat and exhaled, wondering why Roman had put me in charge in the first place, why I'd accepted. Why I'd made the decisions I'd made. Why we'd come over a thousand miles on such a fool's errand. What I was going to tell the others back in Issaquah ...

"If we could ... if we could just *move* faster, maybe," I said. "Get there before anything could triangulate us."

Mr. Fantastic only shook his head. "No, man. *No.* You're smarter than that. Turn us around, Jamie. Turn us around ... and let's go home."

I took off my glasses and rubbed the bridge of my nose.

At length Sam said, "I can drive—if you're not up to it. I don't mind, really."

I must have nodded. All I remember for certain is hearing the engine start and Lazaro grumbling before Nigel said, unexpectedly, "Wait a minute. Wait a minute. *The Ranch.*"

"Forget it," I said—irritably. I didn't want to hear it, whatever it was.

"Holy shit, I forgot all about it." I heard the map rattle as he tapped it. "The Ranch. The Ranch, mon, Sunset Ranch."

Lazaro cursed as he swiveled in his chair. "What the fuck are you even—"

"What do mean, 'Sunset Ranch?'" I glanced at the map and quickly back to him. "Talk to me, dammit!"

He only shrugged, carelessly, nonchalantly. "It— it's a tourist attraction, sort of a barbeque joint, but with a riding stable and a corral full of horses. It's right here." He indicated a spot on the map. "Yuh, see, there's even a trail, here, which intersects with Mount Lee Drive."

"And follow that right into an ambush?" Mr. Fantastic harrumphed.

"Horses," I muttered. "Holy *Christ.*"

I slouched over the map and pointed. "If there's horses left alive we could follow the trail to Mount Lee Drive and then cross it—right here, then cut through the hills north by northwest until we come straight to the bunker." I looked at everyone one by one. "Not only that, but if we get attacked ... they'll go for the horses. Not us."

I tried to smile as Sam glowered at me. "More meat," I said, and shrugged.

The cockpit fell silent as everyone thought about it.

"I've never even rode a horse," said Mr. Fantastic. "How the hell am I going to—"

"You'll stay with *Gargantua,*" I said. "And cover us with the .50 cal for as far as you can. How about the rest of you?"

"4-H Blue-ribbon, Poulsbo State Fair," said Sam. "2007."

"Used to ride 'em right there at Sunset," said Nigel, "when we were working for Eagleton."

I looked at Lazaro, who seemed to hesitate.

"Of course I've ridden a fucking horse," he grumbled. "I'm from Idaho." He added: "What about you?"

"Never in my life," I said, and looked at Sam—I don't know why. "But I'll manage. Don't worry about it."

I looked at Mr. Fantastic, who just shook his head.

"Okay ..." I breathed. I held my hand out to the others, palm down. "Who's in?"

And Sam slapped her hand over mine, after which Nigel slapped his hand over her's—and Lazaro topped us all off.

"Great," said Mr. Fantastic, disappointed. "All right ..." He picked up the targeting goggles. "Let's hope there's some horses."

And then we were off, making a U-turn in the middle of Canyon Lake Drive and rumbling toward Sunset Ranch—all of us, I think, wondering if we were really up to it, and if we could actually pull it off. All of us, I think, frightened out of our wits.

As it turned out, there *were* horses: fourteen of them, to be exact, all of which were healthy and had been well-maintained—thanks to a woman named Shawna, who lived at the Ranch. Nor had our meeting been a confrontational one, in part because she'd been riding out in the field when we'd first rumbled up and had hardly been in a position; but mostly because she was a woman of singular grace and beauty who wouldn't have hurt a fly—even if her life and wellbeing had depended on it. In this case, fortunately—it hadn't.

"Well now, if that isn't a posse," she said, and took the picture—even as our horses grew restless and mine most of all: nickering and neighing, clearly wanting to go. "The Apple Dumpling Gang rides again."

She waited as the Instamatic developed the snapshot and pushed it out—humming in the silence, groaning as though its batteries were low. "Ah, see?"

She quickly approached and handed it to me. "That'll be a buck ninety-eight."

I took it but didn't look at it yet, smiling down at her from "Rusty," liking the way the sun fell on her face and hair. "Just add it to your Lifetime Protection Plan," I said, and glanced at *Gargantua.* "You're going to like having that parked here, I think."

"If it means I'll be seeing you again, I will," she said, and beamed up at me, earnestly, unguardedly. She seemed to grow somber. "Take care of my horses, Jamie. Bring them back safe."

I looked at the picture, which showed the four of us mounted in front of the trailhead, our rifles slung across our backs—and smiled. "I will do everything in my power, Shawna. I prom—" I left off, feeling as though a cold hand had gripped my heart. *"Oh, no."* I looked from the picture to the trail.

"What is it?" Her previously lilting voice had lowered an octave. "What's wrong?"

I gripped the reins, dropping the picture—even as Rusty whinnied and squirmed—wanting to reach back and unsling my rifle; wanting to have some kind of defense. But it was already too late; too late for fight or flight. Too late for anything but to hold perfectly still. *"Shhh,"* I whispered, "nobody move. And don't reach for your weapons. Don't even breathe."

I indicated the trail—the horses snorting and shuffling about—even as Shawna followed my gaze, and gasped.

"Oh, my God."

"Shhh ..."

We didn't budge, didn't blink, as the allosaur approached: its leg muscles working beneath black and pebbled skin; its blood-red crests gleaming (for, indeed, it appeared to be the same one we had encountered earlier in the day).

"No way, man," moaned Lazaro—quietly, unsteadily. "No fucking—"

I waved him to silence even as Shawna worked the horses—stroking their manes, rubbing their snouts; trying to calm them—as I recalled something about horses and predators in the wild, something I'd read: which was that they didn't fear predators so much as the *act of predation*—meaning, I suppose, that those who hadn't encountered dinosaurs before (which these hadn't, according to Shawna) would have no reason to fear them—unless, of course, they (the dinosaurs) behaved in a threatening way. Which, curiously, this one wasn't doing.

I carefully reached behind me and pressed the emergency button on my radio. "Here's where we find out if Mr. Fantastic is right ..."

I glanced at Shawna, who looked back at me questioningly.

"About their vision," I said. "Predatory dinosaurs. About it being movement-based."

To the others I mumbled: "I just alerted Mr. Fantastic; we gotta give him time. He'll hear it and then arm the .50 cal. Just hang on. And keep your horses steady."

"Here it comes," said Sam, indicating the allosaur.

And it came—but did not attack; striding instead to a nearby trough (or rather a bathtub on blocks) and beginning to drink—deeply—before plopping down in a cloud of dust and beginning to yawn and stretch ... after which it laid its chin flat and just stared at us—as though we were friends. As though we were one big, happy family.

I exchanged glances with Shawna, who smiled earnestly, unguardedly, even as something whirred—*Gargantua's* .50 cal, which swiveled and lowered, training itself on the allosaur.

I shook my open palm, indicating he shouldn't fire.

"Shawna," I said—breathlessly, tensely—eyeing the animal carefully, "Walk back to your house. Don't be afraid. Just ... walk. Slowly. Non-threateningly. Go."

"Oh, my God, Jamie. But—"

"Do it," I said, feeling for my rifle, touching its wood stock. "We've got you covered." I gripped the weapon and brought it around—slowly, non-threateningly—saw Sam and the others doing the same. To them I said: "Don't fire unless I tell you to."

Lazaro harrumphed, sneering. "What should we do, then, introduce ourselves?"

I looked at the allosaur: at its golden eyes, which were entirely free of the glow—"the Color," as we often called it, the mysterious light by which we always knew an animal had been affected, been swayed, by *them,* by the Others—which seemed almost passive, meditative.

"Easy ... He's not a threat." I watched as Shawna went, cautiously, reluctantly—then motioned again to *Gargantua.*

Do not engage, I repeated, staring at its tinted windows. *Hold your fire.*

"This is ridiculous," cursed Lazaro, and pumped his long gun—slowly, smoothly, with hardly a sound. "Are we going to leave it? What—so it can come after us the moment it starts to feel hungry? Are you kidding?"

But I'd already decided; the allosaur would be spared.

We weren't going to butcher it—even if it meant facing it later, and increasing our risk. Because it was important, somehow—keeping it alive. It was ... I can't explain it, not really—I couldn't then and I can't now. I just knew that we couldn't kill it. That it—had a purpose, somehow. A *mission.* Just as we.

"That's exactly what we're going to do," I said, and patted Rusty's shank, encouraging him forward. "Now let's move."

And we moved, trotting up the orangish-tan clay like Chieftains, like a posse, our rifles in one hand and the reins in the other (the allosaur closing its eyes and seeming to doze as *Gargantua's* cannon hummed and realigned, following us as we went), Shawna watching safely from her window.

It was at once garish and sublime, hipster and gauche, a burnt-orange relic of a bygone era with a tip of the hat to Frank Lloyd Wright and a debt to Googie architecture—a thing as righteous as it was ridiculous, which sat amongst its desert like an outsider, an intruder, as out of place as the transplanted palms and piped-in water, as artificial as L.A. itself.

"They weren't kidding when they called it the Lost Aztec Temple of Mars," I said, as Rusty fidgeted and nickered, and shook flies from his ears. "But what's with all the high fencing and concertina wire—only to leave the entire front-perimeter open? There's just a hedgerow. No fence at all."

Nigel sat up in his saddle and looked on, the sweat beading along his forehead. "Be damned if I know; it wasn't like that before." He looked around the area—skittishly, I thought. "Maybe he had it removed when they took out the road. He was like that, you know. All about the visual." He pointed at the house itself. "Wouldn't have been a problem, though, even if it *were* there—there's a man door in the fence just beyond that breezeway."

I held out my arm as everyone started to move. "I—hold up. I—ah, I don't like this."

I scanned the overgrown yard and the cosmetically-placed boulders (some of which were the size of moving vans); looking for traps, looking for threats. "It doesn't feel right."

Lazaro got off his horse and approached the hedgerow—then turned to face us, splaying his arms. "What? You heard Jamaica; dude was all about the visual. Probably figured there was no need—once the road was taken out. For a front fence, I mean." He let his arms slap to his sides. "Now are we going to go check it out, or what? Or are you all just going to sit there all day?"

And there was a growling noise, a deep-throated snarl, which sounded from behind one of the rocks even as a shadow fell across the knee-high grass—at which a great cat padded out which was easily the size of a pickup, and *hissed* at us: its huge pallet showing pink and pale, its black lips stretching, its whiskers and curved fangs—which were like tusks—gleaming in the sun.

"Lazaro, *don't!*"

But it was too late; he'd already drawn his pistol and squeezed off a few rounds—which went *pop, pop, pop* in the late afternoon sun and echoed along the hills; which reverberated across the valley like the sound of a car backfiring.

"Goddammit, man," I cursed, even as my horse and everyone else's leapt up in a panic and started to bolt; as Lazaro's trotted into the scrub and didn't look back, as the saber-toothed cat advanced several yards toward us—and stopped.

"You—you just let that entire army know we're still here; and exactly where we're at," I snapped, having wrestled my horse back around along with everyone else (although Nigel was still struggling), and finally climbed off, tossing the reins into the scrub. I looked at the cat, the Smilodon, which paced back and forth furiously. "Now just back away, *slowly. And hold your fire.* It's not advancing. Come on!"

But he didn't; back away, that is—all least not right away; choosing instead to creep closer ... advancing several feet before pausing in front of the hedgerow and leaning forward—looking down.

"Yo, Jamie! You got to see this!" He turned to face us, his face lit up like a child's. "Come on! It's completely safe."

I looked at Sam, who got off her horse and looked back at me—tentatively, hesitantly. And then we moved forward, Nigel having gained control of his steed and dismounted and quickly run up to join us.

"It's a moat," said Lazaro, "like the kind they have at Woodland Park. Check it out."

I looked into its depths, amazed at its cleverness and ingenuity; at its ability to follow form with function.

"A perfect illusion," I said, shaking my head, and added: "Leave it to a sci-fi writer, I guess. To come up with something like this." I peered through the breezeway at the house, which seemed wide open to us now. "My friends ... it is time."

I looked at the others and then to Sandahl—to Sam. "Let's go check out the world's most well-appointed basement, shall we?"

"It's more than that," she said, and beamed; our beautiful and only female (in the away team, that is, since we'd lost Joan); our very own Heather Locklear. "It's home."

And then there was a burst of gunfire and she fell—just slouched face-first into the dirt; and we all followed the sound to the Hollywood sign where an array of trucks had fanned out above and behind it—all along the ridge—trucks with blue and white flags flying from their beds.

After which we scooped Sam up by her armpits and scrambled for the nearest rock formation: where Nigel and Lazaro began shooting back while I leaned over Sam and the blood poured from her mouth and down her cheeks. Where it trickled into the orangish-tan clay even as she looked up at me—trying but failing to form words; trying to tell me something but wholly unable—and pooled around her head like dark, red wine.

"Jesus, Jamie, *look.*"

It was Nigel—catching his breath with his back to the rocks, peering beyond the hedgerow. I followed his gaze to where the cat had begun backing up—crouched low like a puma, swinging its hindquarters. Focused on us like a laser beam.

"Jesus, shoot it!" I snapped, cradling Sam's head in my arms, unable to do it myself. "Hurry, before it—"

But it was too late—the Smilodon had already launched itself at the moat: clearing it but only barely, snatching the hedgerow in its forepaws, fighting its way up and over.

And then we were pinned: Nigel and Lazaro firing at the Tucker train as I cradled Sam and the Smilodon approached; as the Communications Center exploded and there was a tremendous fireball—which rose, curling, into the clear, blue sky— as the cat hunkered down yet again (as if to pounce) but was disrupted by a hiss and a snarl from behind me; from behind the rock formation, at which the black allosaur stalked out and crouched low—its foreclaws splayed, its eyes rolling back in its skull— and launched itself at the cat—like a cobra, almost, or a barracuda—the force of it spinning the tiger in the dust and pushing it onto its back, where it thrashed and snapped its teeth—but quickly rebounded.

I snatched up my radio and toggled it: *"Gargantua One* this is Mobile, do you copy?"

Sam stirred as I waited, reaching up and touching my face, trying desperately to speak, as guns crackled all around us.

"Gargantua, go ahead."

"Listen up: We are pinned down at the bunker and are taking heavy fire. I need you to double-time it back to the gate and engage those targets. Engage them—and then move right up the road, all the way to the Communications Center. Use your smoke screen; it'll disorient them. But you need you to hit 'em with everything you got, understand? *Gargantua. Do you copy?*"

I heard it across the hills even before he acknowledged: the rapid-fire of *Gargantua's* Gatling gun—tearing up targets, hopefully taking out the missile operator.

The radio hissed and squelched. "I heard it and I am already there, *and* engaging," said Mr. Fantastic. "Stand by."

I put my hand over Sam's own and held it against my cheek, holding her as tight as I could, rocking her gently. "Hang in there, kiddo. We're going to get you to that medical bay, you just wait and see. *But you've got to hang in there.*"

I watched as the animals spun around in a deathmatch, kicking up orange dust, causing clouds of it to overtake us, growling and gnashing their teeth.

"It's no good, mon," said Nigel. "I'm down to my last clip."

"Here," said Lazaro, and tossed him a fresh one. "I brought extra."

But Nigel was right: We weren't going to last, much less get Sam to a medical bay—not the one in *Gargantua* and not the one in the bunker. I just didn't see it happening before—

Before—

And there was a sound, very faint at first but growing, intensifying, coming closer. Getting louder—and I mean exponentially. Chopping the air like a string of firecrackers, like a machete, seeming to eclipse everything as a shadow passed over the ground and I peered skyward—following the thing as it briefly blotted the sun, tracking it as it pounded toward the Hollywood sign.

A helicopter. An Apache. The most beautiful thing I had ever seen, before or since. Our own Roman Malone—Black Stringfellow Hawke, as he jokingly referred to himself (in deference to Mr. Fantastic and that old TV show, *Airwolf*). Our Eye in the Sky—who had gone into Fort Lewis and come out with a tiger in his pocket. Who had somehow managed the impossible and brought it all the way here—to save us in our most desperate hour; to save Sam before she bled out.

"Well hello down there," came his familiar voice over the radio—followed by a loud burst of static, which crackled and popped. "Looks like you've made some friends here already ..."

I watched as he circled the mountain: being a good Eye in the Sky, taking in the lay of the land. "Is that something I might be of assistance with? We got rockets."

"Hot-damn, that crazy bastard did it," shouted Lazaro—gripping Nigel's shoulder, giving it a shake.

"Flyboy comes through again!" He howled at the sky.

"We're the posse that can't be stopped, man," said Nigel, and gripped him back. "The Issaquah Five has struck again. Can you believe it, James? I mean, can you—"

But I wasn't looking at him anymore, Sam's hand having relaxed and slid slowly from my cheek, her head having slumped, heavily, it seemed, deeper into my arms.

"Is she—?" began Nigel, as Lazaro grimaced.

"Fuck no, man ..."

But she was gone, and there was nothing else to say.

Nothing else to do.

I lowered her to the dirt—slowly, gingerly—as small arms continued to rattle and pop. Nor did I notice the absence of combat from the animals—although, looking back, it must surely have been over. Nobody said anything for several moments.

At last my radio squelched. "Jamie, this is *Gargantua*—and the road has been cleared ... to within about a quarter mile of the Communications Center. I can see it from my location. Thing is, that Apache's got them seriously spooked, and they seem to be heading out ... heading this way. What do you want me to do, over."

But I just remained slumped over Sam, feeling responsible for it—all of it—feeling as though I'd failed her. Feeling as though I was to blame.

"Second that, Jamie," came Roman, followed by another burst of static. "We got them in a pincer, a real kill box. This is your call."

I looked at Nigel and Lazaro, my eyes brimming with tears.

"We'll have to deal with them eventually, Jamie," said Nigel—softly. "I think you know that as well as I do."

I must have focused on Lazaro, who said, "Take it from someone who knows them. They'll be back."

At last I toggled the mic: "Sam is dead," I said, and gave it a moment to sink in. "So here's what we're going to do. Mr. Fantastic, I want you to hold the line and prevent any of them from escaping, okay?" I waited for him to acknowledge. "But it's going to fall on you, Roman, to neutralize them. Because they're too dangerous to leave standing. Just ... use everything you have. There's no children. There are, however, woman and young people. It— it's a tribe, you understand Like ours. But—they've made it clear: we're not welcome. Nobody is. Under penalty of execution. And they've claimed all of Hollywood." I looked at Sandahl's lithe, crumpled form. "And, well ... they killed Sam."

I lowered the radio and stood, now that the firing had stopped, and looked at the ridge, where the Tucker trucks were evacuating. "This one's for you, Sam." Then I raised it again. "Play something for her, would you, *Gargantua?* The Randy Newman album. And pipe it over the loudspeakers so we can hear it. Otherwise ... fire when ready."

And then we waited, watching the trucks with their billowing flags slowly move along the ridge, watching them go.

Last night I saw Lester Maddox on a TV show / With some smart-ass New York Jew / The Jew laughed at Lester Maddox / And the audience laughed at Lester Maddox too ...

I heard gunshots—nothing major, just some idiot in the Tucker train shooting at the sky.

So I went to the park and I took some paper along / And that's where I made this song ...

And then it started, the Apache firing two Hellfire missiles which hit a group of pickups at the start of the train and instantly blew them to pieces, glass and shrapnel flying, a body tumbling in the air.

We talk real funny down here / We drink too much, we laugh too loud / We're too dumb to make it in no northern town ...

Two more missiles fired, this time at the other end of the train, blowing pickups and blue flags into the air, sending a cab higher than anything else—like the turrets of those Iraqi tanks in the first Gulf War—hurling a Rugged Terrain tire along the ridge, which eventually rolled down the hill.

We're keeping the niggers down ...

More missiles, like scaled-up bottle rockets: hitting the column like hammers, making fireballs of King Cabs and beds of people; spitting from the chopper's hardpoints like fireworks, like flairs, incinerating skin and catching hair on fire, I knew, and didn't care, obliterating pennants and banners.

We're rednecks, we're rednecks / We don't know our ass from a hole in the ground ...

Until he'd finally fired everything: Hellfires and Hydras, Stingers and Spikes, all of them hissing and screaming, finding their targets; all of them lighting the ridge up like the Fourth of July, or maybe the volcano at The Mirage, in Las Vegas, each making our world safer and saner and more secure—more righteous, more lost.

Each bringing smoke and silence and peace—like the lights in the sky themselves—to the war-torn hills of Earth.

By the time Roman had finished mopping up and landed the Apache, we'd covered Sam with a tarp from *Gargantua* (Mr. Fantastic had parked it next to the Hollywood sign) and I'd closed the allosaur's eyes—having said a prayer for him first in appreciation of his sacrifice (for he'd surely saved us from the saber-toothed cat, which also lay dead) and even piled stones.

"I don't know why he took to us like that," said Lazaro, walking over to join me, "but I'm sure glad he did."

We looked down at the beast as the sun continued to sink and everything took on a golden hue.

"You were right, you know. About not killing him." He looked at me as the breeze tousled his hair. "And I'm sorry."

I stared at the allosaur, which looked oddly at rest, oddly peaceful, and thought about Sam. "Yeah. Well. I was wrong about a lot of things too."

I looked up to see Roman walking toward us across the scrub. "If that look means what I think it does you can knock it off, right now," he said, and paused. "We all knew the danger; Sam perhaps most of all. She died doing what she believed." He looked at the allosaur and then to me. "Don't take that away from her."

I rested my hand on his shoulder. "Nor you, Roman?"

He straightened suddenly and looked me in the eye. "Nor me. We both did exactly what we had to do." He gripped my shoulder and shook it slightly.

"It wasn't the first time, as you'll recall. And it won't be ..."

I must have squinted at him. "What? What is it?"

But he only stared beyond me—toward the bunker, toward the breezeway, at which I turned around and saw an old man creeping toward us holding a shotgun: a man as bloated and pale, as unhealthy, as I had ever seen; a man in silk pajamas and a monogramed bathrobe, who's dark hair was parted as if with a knife and who wore yellow-tinted glasses through which you could clearly see his eyes—a man I instantly recognized as Hugo Eagleton.

"Take off your weapons," he said, continuing to approach, "All of you. *Right now.*"

But nobody did, only moved back slowly to give him space—holding their arms at their sides, ready for anything.

"I'll fill you full of shot, don't think I won't. Now drop 'em. *Now.*" He hurried toward me suddenly, I have no idea why, and stuck the shotgun in my chest. "Who's in charge here? Huh? Is it you, you bespectacled little shit? Answer me!"

"It—it is," I said, sensing everyone stirring, and added, "Everybody just chill, okay? I'm all right."

He used the double barrels to raise my chin. "I'll be the judge of that. Now, listen. I want you to say something—all right? I want you to prove to me you're *human.* Got it? It can be anything; a quote from a book, a humorous aphorism, a dirty joke; hell, we can have a Socratic dialogue, for all I care. Just entertain and enlighten me; prove to me you're human and not one of these animals wandering the city like a saw-boned coyote—just looking for something to eat. *Or fuck.* And make it snappy, yeah? 'Brevity is the soul of wit,' they say. I don't have time to dawdle—one look at me should tell you that." He pushed the shotgun hard against my throat. "And go. You're the Oracle at Delphi."

I rolled my eyes, looking around. "Nobody try anything, all right? I—I got this. I think." I took a deep breath and exhaled. "Okay. Fine." I cleared my throat. "The Dreaming City ... by Hugo Eagleton. Ch-chapter One, paragraph one." I paused to collect my thoughts. 'It ... it was the first night of the Sacrificium, a night of sacrifice and death, a night when the black coins tendered in the Lottery would be tendered back. B-but it ... it was also the *Hora Mil—Mille Semitis,* the Hour of a Thousand paths, for that is the day the Sacrificium had fallen on this year, an hour when best friends might become enemies, when lovers of longstanding might betray oaths, in which anything and everything was possible. A night—in other words—for dreaming; but also for something else. Something elusive but impossible to ignore—nebulous—but as real as the River Dire; and which seemed to have stolen into the world on the wind itself ..."

I opened my eyes—having closed them in order to concentrate—and saw that he was crying. Weeping.

"Bullocks, of course," he said, finally, and lowered the shotgun. "Pure, undiluted bullocks—as stupid and naïve as the young man who wrote it."

He let the weapon fall to his side. "Ah, well. Such are the things men busy themselves with." He cocked his head as though thinking of something, as though it were standing right it front of him, whatever it was. "And yet the thing is, I can still remember when I wrote that. Isn't that the damndest thing? It was in that first shithole apartment in New York, the one in Flatbush, Brooklyn." He smiled a little, thinking about it. "Susan was there, still young, still beautiful, but had long since fallen asleep. I was wearing comfortable shoes—funny I should remember that—and I'd eaten not long before. Nothing fancy, just—food that fit my stomach. And there was a good dog; Bruno, a Bull Terrier, laying right at my feet. And that part—that part was not bullocks. That part—well, it's what I should have been writing about, isn't it?"

He looked at me somberly, lucidly. "You're here for the bunker ... aren't you?"

I just nodded, slowly, firmly.

"And if I don't freely give it, I suppose you'll take it—isn't that about right? That about it?"

I nodded again, slowly.

He looked at the dead; at the allosaur and the Smilodon, which must have been some sort of pet, and poor Sam, with one foot sticking out of her tarp.

"Is this all of you? Just you five? There's no women? No kids?"

"There's 28—27—of us ... in total," I said. "Got a settlement in Issaquah ... that's in Washington State, at an old drive-in theater. It's been good, but ... we're running out of things. Out of supplies. And it's getting harder and harder to make excursions into the city, into Seattle. It, ah, it gets more treacherous every day. We ... we've lost a lot of good people."

He seemed to think about that, scratching at his stubble. He leaned forward abruptly. "There's food enough here to last a decade," he said, conspiratorially. "Maybe longer. Not to mention the hydroponics, and a modest medical facility. *There's even a bowling alley.*"

"We'd love to see it," I said. I looked at Sam. "But I don't want to leave her like that. Do you have a shovel—or a spade? Maybe some blankets? Or a pillow?"

He reached up and gripped my shoulder—the dude was definitely short—gave it a little shake.

"Son, we'll give your friend all the honors she deserves, and more, or my name isn't Hugo Eagleton." He slapped my arm harder than was necessary. "You just follow old Uncle Hugo to the shed."

And then we went, Lazaro, Nigel, Mr. Fantastic, Roman, and I, through the orange breezeway and into the back yard—which was populated with stone beasts—into his private world; which he'd decided to share.

Needed to share, I'm certain.

IN THE SEASON OF KILLING BOLTS

A tale from the beginning of the Flashback

"Good morning, Sandy Chain Peninsula, and it's Thursday once again—Thursday the 25th of November, in case you were wondering—one day closer to Friday; and this is your Morning Catch of news, weather, and interviews—not to mention great music—with me, Mollie Vaughan. Now, as we all know, yesterday was a real Debbie-downer: gray, chill, and damp. The good news is that today is looking better—with a high of 72 and winds south at 5 to 10 mph, with a low around 55. And, while the sun may give way to rain this afternoon—with a 20 percent chance of precipitation—winds are expected to remain calm, at around 9 mph. All of which is my way of saying that what I hope to do today through the magic of radio is to lift your hearts, your moods, and your limbs—is that asking too much at 6:01 am? I guess we'll find out as we anticipate our main event: an exclusive, in-studio interview with Deputy Bennet Firth—19-year veteran of the Sandy Chain Police Department and winner of the 2017 Mayor's Choice Award—that you're not going to want to miss. It's all coming up at the bottom of the hour; but first, the news ..."

I looked at Bennet and he looked back, coolly, nonchalantly. "What? It's not like it's a big deal, you know. I mean—Jesus. You'd think the town has never called on me before."

I glanced at his badge, which had been buffed to a spirited shine, and his pressed Khakis; at his glossy black belt and shoes. "Oh, I just thought you might be anxious, that's all. I reckon I should have known."

I returned my attention to the clipboard, which I'd braced against the wheel. "I'm sure Mollie will ensure everything goes to spec. I mean, she runs a tight ship, Mollie. A tight, fine—"

"Look, I don't want to hear about her tight, fine ship, all right?" He glanced at the roses on the dash—a subtle accusation. "I just want to get through this. And—and to assure Sandy Chain we're on duty. Both of us. Still."

By which he meant to say: Because some of us have remained focused—know what I mean, 'Chief?' On the needs of the community, on good, old-fashioned police-work. On our duty, if you don't mind; and on service, not grieving endlessly, endlessly—or worse, acting like teenagers. Not dwelling on personal matters.

I finished scribbling in my log. "We're here," I agreed—and tossed the clipboard onto the dash. "Still. Now let's get some coffee ... and you to the station."

And then I started the patrol truck and put it in gear—but paused, distracted, looking at the still-dark horizon, looking beyond the breakers. "There's no raincloud out there," I said. "Nothing but clear sky."

"Yeah, well, I wouldn't be so sure," said Bennet. "Oh, I know, everyone says July, or August, maybe September, but in my experience, it's November. November's the season—the season of killing bolts. You just mark my words."

And I did—mark his words, that is. Marked them and filed them away: under hyperbole. Under 'how to speak with grandiloquence.' Under Shit My Deputy Says.

I had to hand it to her, I thought, even as we entered Carmichael's and Cecilia rushed to turn down the radio; she (Mollie) knew how to sound objective even when reporting on things I knew pissed her off: "... America's allies are calling to congratulate President-elect Jon Brady even as President Tucker refuses to concede the election; among them President Emmanuel Macron of France and Prime Minister Boris Johnson of the United Kingdom. Tucker meanwhile has not publicly conceded and continues to make claims of election rigging and voter fraud ..."

"Cecilia; I don't know how you even hear them bells with such an infernal racket going on." I motioned for her to remain seated even as we made our way toward the coffee urns. "Nah, nah. You just sit right down there and give little Archie a chance to breathe, you hear?"

She blushed and dropped a hand to her bump, which was more of a basketball. "Little Archie—" And she tittered. "Not X Æ A-Xii—like Steve Dannon and Sharona?"

"The rich can afford to be weird," said Bennet. He took a Styrofoam cup and began to fill it. "Like that Hugo Eagleton—the guy who wrote The Sleeping City, or whatever. Named his kid 'Rocket.' I mean, can you imagine? A kid named 'Rocket?'" He snickered through his nose. "Going to have to teach that kid how to fight; that's all I have to say."

I filled my own cup and went to the counter, took out my debit card. "Oh, I don't know. I kind of like it. It's got—how do you say it? Gravitas." I looked at Cecilia. "I've got these, darling. Can't have Bennet paying for his own coffee, not today; he's the man of the moment!"

Bennet just shrugged. "It's nothing, really. Little PR for the Department." He lifted his chin and squared his shoulders. "People see things like the race riots in Seattle and, well, they get scared—that's all. Just need to know there's a firm hand at the wheel."

Cecilia nodded slowly, tentatively. "So are you ... going to be on television? Or on the radio?"

"Oh, radio; radio. KEXM, right next door. You'll—you'll be able to hear the whole thing." He hitched up his Khakis briskly. "Yeah, just something a lawman has to do ... I mean, now and again. Touch base with his public. Let 'em know he's on the beat." He laughed a little. "After all, we work for you, right? I mean, it sure isn't the reverse. I can tell you that."

"Speaking of which," I indicated the clock on the wall. "Isn't it about that time?"

"Is it?" Bennet looked at the big IBM. "Well—so it is." And to Cecilia: "Well. Reckon that's why I don't currently have a lady friend. Married to duty, as they say."

"Aww. Well, break a leg," she said.

"Yep ..." He exhaled loudly. "My lady is Sandy Chain."

"Bennet."

And we went—as Cecilia refused to run my card (as usual) and the radio blared (with Mollie talking about a bold new era in human achievement and the imminent return of Steve Dannon's Daedalus Seven spacecraft) and the door chimed and the wind—which had picked up markedly, alarmingly, inexplicably—met our faces.

"Chief Townsend! Hey, wait!"

I turned to see Vicki from Blevins Pharmacy rushing up the sidewalk.

"Am I glad to see you!" She paused to catch her breath, the hair whipping and lashing her face—before extending a white bag. "Tell me you'll deliver this to Wilber Cole—out in Mirabeau Park—like, yesterday, please? Before he eats anything?"

I took the bag and looked at her. "Now you know that when you ask like that I can't help but to comply." I peeked inside the sack. "I'm not even going to ask."

"One in the morning—before breakfast, and one at night, just before dinner." She jumped as a garbage can toppled and papers cycloned. "Before meals, okay? Don't forget."

"It'll be done—I was going out there anyway. Go on, git."

She paused, looking suddenly abashed. "Oh, Chief—"

"It's all right," I watched as the power lines began to waver—ominously, precariously. "Vicki, don't make me—"

And she went; as Bennet and I crossed the street to the station and went up to its double doors—where he paused, abruptly. "Look, Archie. Maybe we should—"

"Aw, no. I won't hear of it. Now you've been looking forward to this all week. So just go in there and knock 'em dead—and I'll see you on the other side."

"Aw, Arch, but what if—"

"No, no. Everything out here is gonna to be fine." I nodded once, twice. "Go on. Make us proud."

He moved to go in but hesitated. "You don't even have your service revolver; now when are you going to get back on the horse, anyway? I mean, I'm sorry, Arch, but someone has to say it. It's time for you to snap out of it."

I scanned the trees, which were leaning in the wind, and the brownstone buildings, whose screens rattled. "Just a storm. Don't need a revolver for that."

"Yeah, well. You'd think better if, say, the Dusty Moths—"

"Who aren't going to be riding around in a storm; I can guarantee it. Now go on."

And he went on, shaking his balding head, which shined like his badge, slamming the door behind him—after which I heard a rap on the glass above and looked up; saw Mollie holding a sign against one of the second-story windows, a sign which read, simply: NIGHTCAP AT MIDNIGHT JOE'S?

At which I just smiled and gave her a thumbs up.

"Yeah, well, sure, I try to stay sharp. And that means a lot of time at the range—lot of time sighting paper targets. (laughter) I mean, I'm no Jingo Williams—you ever seen him? Jingo Williams? On TV, I mean? Him and that Oriental gal? Amazing. Amazing shootist. I saw him do a trick once where he—"

I switched off the ignition and sighed, rubbed the bridge of my nose. 'Oriental.' I got out and shut the door.

Oreo was already there, barking and slavering, his white paws on the fence. Greeting me as he greeted everyone, with a hail of yaps and spit.

I shook him by a jowl. "Whoos a good boy? Whoos a good boy?"

"Not that dog," snapped Wilber, drawing my attention (to the porch, yes, but also to the fact that he was wearing nothing but saggy undershorts and a wifebeater). "Not one little bit. Bugger chewed up my lawn gnome. Just chewed it to pieces. Ate its head off! I mean, look at it."

I looked to where he'd indicated; saw a plastic lawn gnome with—sure enough—its head chewed off. "Aw, no." I clicked my heals, saluted smartly. "Wilber. For him the war is over."

Wilber just looked at me. "You, ah, you out here on business, Chief? Or are you just out here to be cute?"

"Actually, Wilber," I walked toward him and handed him the bag, which crinkled. "I'm here to tell you to take your medicine. Two a day: One before breakfast—one before dinner. Call Vicki with any questions."

He stared at the bag, irritably, contemptuously. "Will it help me sleep?"

"Call Vicki with any questions."

"Hmpf." And he went back inside.

"You're welcome," I said; even as the wind blew and the screen door banged.

And then I looked across the street. At the long, open, swaying gate and the hideous, black, gothic-style arch. At Sandy Chain Community Cemetery with its towering cyclone fences and tombstones like ruined teeth; its brown, semi-frozen lawns; its crypts and sepulchers full of nothing.

Bennet continued as I laid the roses (I'd parked next to her section with the engine running and the door hanging open): "Vacation? (laughter in the studio) No, no, not this Deputy. I mean, what would I do? Yeah, yeah; I know: Go to Bluebeard's Cove, right? Or Devil's Gorge. Go bet on the races at Checkered

Flags. Well, that's fine, I suppose—if you're a civilian. If you're not a lawman. But I am lawman, see, and—"

I stood, staring at the marker, staring at the inscription.

"—an oath of service, a promise to protect. And that promise comes before anything; even, I dare say, family—"

I watched as rain began to spot the granite; to stain the marker in ever-increasing blotches—darkening the 'C' in Cynthia, punctuating the still-fresh epigraph.

"—well, that's true, I don't. I don't. I mean, unless you count Barney; that, he's my dog. Norwegian Elkhound. (proud chuckling) That's the national dog of Norway—"

I stared at the marker.

Were you really so unhappy—so lost? So alone? Was it really so hopeless—and did you hate me so much—that you would use a piece of me—a piece of my work—to at last finish what the pills and alcohol couldn't? Had I abandoned you to that extent, my love? And did any of it—any of it—ever really happen?

I looked at the granite and the semi-frozen grass—the insufficient inscription, the red, wet roses in cellophane.

Where are you, my love, and just as importantly, where am I? Because I no longer care about what I cared about—and so fiercely! while you were here; by which I mean, what I took from you and gave to Sandy Chain, what I thought was my duty but was in fact only selfishness.

I looked up, the rain spotting my eyes, to find the clouds virtually racing.

Where are you, and just as importantly, where am I?

And then I turned toward the west, toward the sea—I'm still not sure why; and became, in that very instant, a kind of statue, a kind of oak. Then I saw the Anomaly for the very first time (that churning, boiling stormfront; that amorphous Man o' War spreading, ink-like, across the sky), and, unable to comprehend what I was seeing, just stood there, frozen, like I'd looked on Medusa herself. Like I'd become Irit; the Lady of Gomorrah—and prideful spouse to Lot—after she'd been turned into a pillar of salt.

"Looks like a mushroom cloud—only, like, horizontal."

I confess I jumped, and that my hand dropped to my weapon—had I carried one. "Donovan. Now how many times have I told you not to cut through the cemetery?"

"Ah, Chief, but then I've got to go all the way around. And there's a mean dog on Oberlin; you know that. Besides," He stepped up next to me and gazed at the cloud. "You don't really mean to tell me you care about that when there's, well, that. Am I right?"

I peered at the cloud: at its curtains of rain and lightning—like the tendrils of a jellyfish—at its billowing cumulonimbus, which flickered and flashed.

"What is that?" I mumbled. "Is that, is that lightning up there, or something?"

I guess he must have followed my gaze. "Up there? Near the top? No—no, I don't think so. More like—more like balloon beacons, or aircraft. Their wing lights, maybe—glowing in the gloom. Those colors, though. They don't—they don't look right. Almost like—"

"That's because you've never seen them," I said, and toggled my radio. "No one has. K-94, this is the Chief. Do you copy?"

But there was nothing—only static. Only white noise. I listened for the truck's radio: nothing. Just dead air. Just silence as thunder rumbled and the rain fell and the wind gusted—powerfully. Alarmingly.

"K-94, this is the Chief—do you copy?"

More static, more noise. I looked at the fast-approaching cloud.

"Donovan," I said.

"Yeah, Chief?"

"Don't cut through the cemetery."

And then I hustled for the truck and quickly climbed in—jammed it into gear, activated the light bar. Then I was driving out of the cemetery at a dizzying clip; reaching for my cellphone even as it started ringing and ringing; glancing at the shotgun as it lay—bleakly, funereally, like a coffin—between the seats.

"What do you mean, gone?" The wipers went squirk, squirk, squirk. "She's probably in the restroom, Hank." I cradled the cellphone as I drove. "I mean, she is pregnant. Jesus. Give her a minute."

"I've given her about 20 minutes—and I'm telling you, she's not here. Now are you coming to check it out, or what?"

"Look, my phone's been ringing since I left Mirabeau; okay? Just hold on. I'm turning onto Main now."

I turned the corner even as a tangle of powerlines cascaded onto the street—spitting sparks, sniping like snakes. "And tell Clayton we've got lines down; front of the pharmacy—Oliver and Maine." I maneuvered around the lines and accelerated. "Tell 'em to hustle."

And then I was pulling up to Carmichael's and ratcheting the break; piling out of the cab even as Hank met me out front and I blew right past him—thankful the place had power, making a beeline for the restroom. Then I was rapping on its thin door even as Hank crowded me from behind and rain pounded the roof.

"Cecilia! Hey! You all right?" I rattled the door handle furiously—locked, of course. "Cecilia! Now, listen, you're going to have to say something, darlin', or we're just going to have to kick this here door right in; ya understand?"

I leaned closer as something seemed to shift; to move—as clothing ruffled and rain trickled. "Cecilia?"

And then it came: Then she screamed, although it wasn't so much a scream as a shriek, a wail—an extended howl the likes of which I'd never heard (and pray I never hear again). Then she was yowling like an animal even as I stepped back and kicked in the door; as I found her hunched over the toilet and starting to mumble-pitifully, incoherently. Defeatedly.

As I rushed in and knelt beside her, turned her to face me—not yet noticing the obvious; not yet noticing the mortal difference, the cruel jest that had been played on her. "Cecilia-what, what is it? What-"

But then I did notice it; noticed her flat stomach, her thin, gaunt face. Her haunted, terror-stricken eyes—and, also, the complete lack of blood anywhere.

"What happened here?"

"No-nothing—nothing happened. Don't you see? He was just—he was just here, inside, kicking ... and then—then the kicking stopped." She batted the tears from her eyes. "It just stopped; do you understand? It—"

She turned and retched into the bowl; forcibly, violently—just retched and retched, her entire body shaking.

I looked at Hank—who was already on the phone—then reached up, slowly, and flushed the toilet.

"Now, listen. There's, ah, there's people on the way here who are gonna help us with this—this thing, okay? So, until then, you just lean on the big white telephone here and try not to move—and I mean not a lick. All right? Ya hear?"

And then my phone rang, and, God help me, I had to take it. Then Donovan's girlfriend was on the line demanding to know why I'd made him walk around the cemetery in the middle of a thunderstorm—and that I had better go look for him, and give him a ride, like, yesterday.

Because he hadn't come home yet, she said, and he wasn't answering his phone.

But that wasn't really what alarmed me. No, what alarmed me was: I hadn't made him cut around the cemetery. And then thunder struck somewhere close; krack-kakroom! And I got a move on.

He lay spreadeagled like a ragdoll—like he'd been making a snow-angel—his tongue fat and blue; as if he'd been eating pomegranates—his entrails unspooled. The cumbersome poncho rustled as I dialed my cellphone and waited for it to ring—and ring.

Dammit, Bennet, pick up ...

"Hello, you've reached the personal number of Bennet 'Benny' Firth—Deputy; Sandy Chain Police Department; Badge Number—well, Badge Number 2, I mean, it's a small department—winner of the 2017—"

I hung up and looked at the body—at its bloody hands, as though Donovan had been trying to shield his face; at the grass and dirt-turning-to-mud, which—

Well, wasn't that odd.

I knelt and examined the ground—which was soaked in blood and rain. It was almost like—yuh, there; and there. Anterior and lateral support impressions. Nude; no shoes. And toeprints: one, two ... three—just three, with no evidence of a heel, no posterior support at all. Not human, obviously. Not dog. Not bear. More like a fucking ostrich; or—

Ka-crack! Karoom!

I jumped as lightning struck a nearby tree—my heartbeat surely stopping, if only for an instant, my bladder feeling as though it might void right then and there. Then I was up; I was standing, looking at the split trunk and the tree's glowing pulp; looking at the burning branches, which crisped and fell away.

Fire extinguisher ... Dammit, get the fire extinguisher!

And then I was hustling, running for the truck as fast as I could, pausing at Cynthia's grave—or at least where her grave should have been—feeling dazed and disoriented; spying the patrol truck where I'd left it—at Wilber's—sprinting for it only to skid to a stop next to the fence and lean on my knees, panting.

Only to wait there where Oreo would have normally greeted me—just as he greeted everyone— with a hail of yaps and spit—but didn't. Holding and looking at all the blood—then following that blood directly to his doghouse ... to where the poor thing had died half in and half out of its door. Where the poor thing had retreated to lick its mortal wounds and curl up in the cold, familiar straw; to wonder if it had protected its people and its property; to bleed out and die.

There was a crashing sound and I froze—the sound of wood splintering and glass breaking. A sound which had come from behind Wilber's house.

I listened carefully, intently—heard only the wind and the rain, the thunder of lightning, dogs barking in the distance. At last it came again, only muffled somewhat, more muted: another splintering, another breaking of glass. This time, however, it hadn't come from outside. No, this time it had born a kind of echo, a kind of interiority—as though it had originated from an interior space. As though it had originated from inside Wilber's house.

As for what I was thinking as I gripped the shotgun and stepped through the shattered doors, I couldn't tell you. Maybe it was just the fact that it felt good to have it in my hands again—the shotgun, I mean, the Remington 870—"Fat Man," as we called it, our nuclear option—the one Bennet wasn't ever allowed to use. Or maybe it was Mollie's newscast with its mentions of President Tucker's refusal to concede and Steve Dannon's Daedalus Seven returning to Earth, the connection being—I suppose—that both of them seemed about as possible as a baby suddenly vanishing or a killer ostrich wandering the peninsula.

Or maybe it was something else entirely; the fact that I'd been so focused on grieving Cynthia (and, paradoxically, perhaps, boning Mollie) that I'd lost track of who I was. It's possible even that, as I raced through Wilber's house armed to the teeth and—having heard something shatter in his bedroom—paused outside his door, I just felt like myself again.

All I know is that all of that went out the window the moment I stepped out and levelled the shotgun—which also happened to be the moment that anything that wasn't, well, whatever that was (although, I confess, having seen Jurassic Park, I had a pretty good idea), simply ceased to exist. Rather, it seemed as though something else took over: something primitive, even primal, something deep within my mammalian DNA. A holdover from when we were frightened, possum-like creatures hiding in the trees, perhaps—an ancestral memory. Wilber, for his part, just slept like the dead.

The thing is that I completely froze as it turned; froze to the extent that I saw every detail of its skin even as I glimpsed Bennet aiming his pistol outside and dove for the floor. As he opened fire and the thing began bouncing off the walls and smashing bookcases, as it thrashed about like a deer I saw on the internet once (which had crashed through the window of a city bus and then proceeded to destroy everything in its path) and basically went insane—reminding me of the crazed deer and yet not, for it was—in the end—a thing utterly without comparison in this world.

A thing which nonetheless wound up in my sights and got blown away—even as Wilber yelped and clasped his ears and Bennet hit the dirt. Which, in the end, only impacted against the wall and collapsed, twitching and convulsing, as I looked outside with my ears still ringing, and, despite the fact that we were on an evergreen peninsula in western Washington State, saw the tops of palm trees swaying in the wind.

That's when I saw them: the people who were left—the shell-shocked survivors of the Flashback (or whatever they call it where you are). That's when I knew that their friends and loved ones had simply vanished—simply ceased to exist—no less than Cecilia's baby—or Cynthia's grave marker; no less than Mollie—who I would come to learn had disappeared during the interview. That's when I knew that Time had melted and that we (and maybe a few others) were all that were and had ever been; that, indeed, the world had been (at least partially) reset to primordia; and that most of those who'd existed, existed no more.

In short, it was when they looked at me and I looked back, knowing my purpose, knowing my role. And finally it was when I patted Wilber on the shoulder and went out—feeling oddly invigorated, oddly at peace. Feeling as though I might yet make a difference—even as I sucked in the post-storm air.

end.

If you enjoyed this work of fiction, please consider leaving a review at your point of sale. Thanks!

www.ingramcontent.com/pod-product-compliance
Lightning Source LLC
Chambersburg PA
CBHW020335160726
47992CB00004B/1851